"It needs some work," Gramps said.

"The whole thing needs work," Hayden said. "I don't know, of course, what you plan to do here, but the fact is that except for Gramps and me and our friends, no one comes here. Sunshine hasn't had any customers for two years now."

It was such a difference from the hustle of Boston. There were no car horns honking. No radios blaring. No one talking.

Livvy stood motionless, letting the nothingness of it all overtake her. She felt tiny and yet part of all creation. The soft breeze lifted and dropped her hair around her cheeks and forehead.

And, as she listened to the sounds of God Himself—the soft splash of the waves, the trill of the birds, the hum of the insects—she fell in love.

"I want it."

In first grade, **JANET SPAETH** was asked to write a summary of a story about a family making maple syrup. She wrote all during class, through morning recess, lunch, and afternoon recess, and asked to stay after school. When the teacher pointed out that a summary was supposed to be shorter than the original story, Janet explained that she didn't feel the readers knew the characters well enough, so she was expanding on what was in the first-grade reader. Thus a writer was born. She lives in the Midwest and loves to travel, but to her, the happiest word in the English language is *home*.

Books by Janet Spaeth

HEARTSONG PRESENTS
HP458—Candy Cane Calaboose
HP522—Angel's Roost
HP679—Rose Kelly
HP848—Remembrance
HP872—Kind-Hearted Woman
HP895—The Ice Carnival
HP941—In the Cool of the Evening

Sunshine

Janet Spaeth

Heartsong Presents

For Kacie, without whom there wouldn't be Sunshine, North Dakota. You are so good for my heart! (And you make the best gravy ever!)

For Greg, my fishing advisor. Leeches, lures, worms—you explained them all, and if you rolled your eyes and sighed, you didn't let me know, and for that, I am eternally grateful.

For Patty, who's been my steadfast friend down this bumpy road of life. How can I ever thank you enough?

For North Dakota, despite your crazy weather—which, to tell the truth, I actually kind of love—you will always be home to me.

> *"If people concentrated on the really important things in life,*
> *there'd be a shortage of fishing poles."*
> *Doug Larson*

A note from the Author:
I love to hear from my readers! You may correspond with me by writing:

Janet Spaeth
Author Relations
PO Box 721
Uhrichsville, OH 44683

ISBN 978-1-61626-337-9

SUNSHINE

Our mission is to publish and distribute inspirational products offering exceptional value and biblical encouragement to the masses.

PRINTED IN THE U.S.A.

one

Sunshine, North Dakota
Population, including barn cats, chickens, and earthworms: 14
Form of government: Benevolent anarchy
Main industry: Fishing. Or thinking about fishing.
Recreational area: Little Starling River
where you might find a sunnie or two.
Entertainment venues: Chasing the cats that chase
the chickens that chase the earthworms.
Selling price: Make an offer. If we take it, that's the selling price.
If we don't take it, that's not it.

Livvy Moore leaned back in her chair and studied the advertisement again. It was charming, certainly a change from the usual text she wrote: "Move-in ready. 3 BRs, 2 bth, full bsmt." But there was something else about this ad.

Maybe, just maybe, this was what she'd been waiting for. This could be it.

In fact, this *had* to be it. Why else would a newspaper from some small town in North Dakota have blown up against the tire of her car in downtown Boston? Neat freak that she was, she had tossed it into her car, intending to recycle it when she got to work. A broken-down panel truck had backed traffic up for blocks, and she was stuck with nothing to read. . . nothing except this newspaper, with this intriguing offer.

It had to be divinely given. Her ideas of God and Jesus and the whole church thing were vague and fuzzy and lovely, but she was willing to give credit where credit was due. God was in charge of the wind, right? God had put the newspaper right where she'd see it, knowing she'd feel compelled to recycle it.

She ran her fingers through her hair, knowing that it didn't do her hairstyle any good but beyond caring. Right now she had more important things to think about.

She loved Boston, she truly did. The hustle and bustle that had attracted her, though, was wearing her down. Her job paid well, but she never seemed to have the time to take advantage of the generous salary and do what she wanted, which was to travel. At the moment, her knowledge of the world was limited to what she saw on her regular drive to and from work, or what she viewed on the Travel Channel before she fell asleep each night.

There had to be more. China. Egypt. Zanzibar. Even North Dakota.

"Olivia, I need you to look over these bids again," her boss said, walking in without knocking. "They're too high for my taste. We can't offer that kind of money for those properties, and don't give me any of your sob stories about somebody's widow or ancient granny. We're not in the charity business, you know. I want them by tomorrow at the open of business, so I hope you don't have plans for the evening." He stopped to frown, obviously pretending that he cared.

"Actually," she said, lifting her chin, "I do have plans." From deep inside herself, she'd found a backbone. She'd never told Mr. Evans no before.

"You can cancel them, I'm sure."

Somewhere in the distance, she was sure she heard the soft swish of swords being drawn. "No, I really can't."

He lowered the papers and stared at her over his half glasses. That look had slain dragons, but it hadn't dealt with a woman holding an ad for Sunshine, North Dakota.

"Excuse me?"

A garden. The vision of a garden snapped into place. A garden with peas and corn and carrots, and a white-painted fence surrounding it. She wanted to feel the rich warmth of dirt on her fingers, and to hear the sharp *ping* of a hammer hitting a nail.

That was not going to happen in Evans Real Estate Management, unless she counted watering the skinny philodendron that trailed sadly along the edge of her desk as gardening, and smacking the broken heel of her shoe back into place as construction.

She stood up, folded the newspaper, and placed it in her bag. "I'm giving my notice."

He shook his head as if he didn't understand. "Notice? Notice of what?"

"I'm leaving."

He laughed, a cold humorless sound that was the cement in the fragile wall of her decision. "Do you have another position? You know we have a non-compete agreement. It had better not be another real estate management company you're going to."

"I'm leaving Massachusetts entirely," she said, reaching for her coat.

"You're going to New York, aren't you?" His eyes narrowed.

"No I'm not. I am going to North Dakota."

"North Dakota? Are you out of your mind? Why, there's

nothing there except buffalo and snow."

"I like buffalo and snow." Snow she'd seen, but the closest she'd come to a buffalo was seeing one on an old nickel—and on Animal Planet.

He leaned against her desk and studied her. "You're serious. You're going."

"I am."

"You'll regret it."

"Not as much as I'd regret staying."

Occasionally one is presented with the opportunity to make a grand exit, and this was it, Livvy knew. With great style and panache, she swept out of the room and down the hall to the elevator, quite aware that he had followed her out a few steps and then stopped, his icy glare at her back.

Once she was in the elevator, she pushed the STOP button, leaned against the cold brass railing, and shook like an aspen leaf.

What had she done? *What had she done?*

&

Hayden Greenwood threw the last piece of lumber onto the pile, swiped the Cooter's Hardware hat from his head, and mopped at the sweat that dripped from his forehead. He'd never perspired like this in his life, but then, he'd never had to do so much hard labor before.

He looked around him and sighed.

Apparently Gramps had never seen a slab of wood he didn't like, judging from the contents of the small blue building behind the café. Possibly the kindest thing to do— for him, anyway—would be to burn this thing to the ground, but he knew his grandfather would never allow that. So here he was, on a perfectly good June day when he could be out fishing, emptying yet another storeroom.

As near as he could figure, whenever Gramps ran out of storage space at the Sunshine Resort, he'd simply built another shed. They dotted the swathe of cleared land behind the café, some red, some yellow, some blue. Hayden had a suspicion that the purpose of this storehouse of lumber was, yes, to build more sheds.

"Grub!" Gramps ambled over to Hayden. His body was bent from years of working hard and falling harder. His back was twisted from the time he had a small accident with a blowtorch and a gas canister, when he'd ended up several feet away from where he'd begun. His left arm crooked at an awkward angle, the souvenir of an accident with a saw. His legs bowed as if he'd spent his life on horseback, when, in fact, Hayden knew that Gramps's stance was due to the beat-up cowboy boots he'd worn for at least twenty years, patched and repatched until little was left of the original shoes. No human could walk in them normally.

"Grub, you're not throwing anything away, are you?"

Only Gramps could get away with the childhood nickname. Anyone else trying to use the hated moniker got a quick poke in the stomach, at least when they were kids. Now that he was a grown-up, he hadn't had to enforce the no-Grub rule, but on the other hand, he didn't really have anyone to fight with.

Plus his fighting days were over. It was like the Bible said. You get to be a man, you put away childish things. And to his way of thinking, that included punching people who called him Grub.

"No, Gramps, I'm not throwing anything away. See these boards? They all came from inside this shed."

The elderly man peered at the stack with eyes that were bleary with age. "I recollect there were more."

"And there are." With Gramps, Hayden always managed to find a well of patience that he didn't really have with the rest of the world. "I'm not finished yet."

"Good thing we're selling this place." Gramps looked away and sniffed. He wiped the back of his hand across his nose before turning back to Hayden. "Too much work for an old codger like me, and not enough to keep the young blood like you here."

It was the end of an era. The CLOSED sign had been hanging on the canteen door for almost two years. The bait shop now held boxes of half-empty BB canisters and rusted fish hooks, left over from the Sunshine Resort's heyday.

There hadn't been much else to the resort. As long as the kids had a place to buy taffy and ice cream during the day and a cleared area for bonfires and marshmallow roasts at night, and the grown-ups had a pier to fish on and a jetty to launch their boats from, all had been good. There was no stress at the Sunshine Resort, not until the lure of places that included shopping as a recreation edged nearer. At the back of his closet, Hayden still had a T-shirt, once orange but now faded to a soft coral, emblazoned with the words: AT THE END OF THE DAY, THERE'S SUNSHINE.

His parents had died when he was ten, and Gramps and Gran had taken him into their hearts and home and provided everything the grieving boy had needed. He could never thank them enough.

He glanced at his grandfather, who seemed tinier than ever before, and his heart contracted painfully. Gramps's health had been steadily failing since Gran had died two years earlier, and he knew it wouldn't be long until God would call the old man home.

Hayden wanted to savor every moment with Gramps.

He cleared his throat. There was only one thing to do.

"Let's go fishing."

ॐ

Livvy moved the monitor of her computer so the last rays of the early summer sunlight didn't glare on it.

"Mom, it's all taken care of," she said to the screen.

"Can't you wait until your father and I can come and help you?" her mother said. "August would be good."

Livvy sighed. Her parents were in Sweden, teaching at a school there, and through the magic of a computer program, they were able to talk. They could even see each other's image as they did it.

It was a mixed blessing. Her father was quiet, the kind of man who listened and absorbed everything, and spoke rarely. Her mother made up for any of his silences. "It'll be fine. I'll be fine," Livvy assured her.

Mrs. Moore shook her head vigorously, the image flickering as the computer tried to keep up with the rapid motion. "Livvy, I can't think this is a good idea. You've got a good job—"

"Had a good job," she interrupted.

"Had a good job," her mother continued. "Livvy, that reminds me. What did you do with the things from your office? If you just walked out—"

"What things from my office?"

"You know, like photos and mementos."

Livvy's laugh was cold. "Photos and mementos were not allowed. We could have one plant, which was replaced regularly because there wasn't enough light to keep anything alive. No, when I left, I think I left some pens, and maybe a sweater and my planner. Nothing too big."

Her mother persisted. "Your apartment is nice. What's going to happen with that? Don't you have a lease?"

Livvy smiled. "Not anymore. The apartment was re-rented by the end of the day. I just have to be out in two weeks."

"What about your furniture?"

"I'm putting some of it in storage. The rest I've donated to that thrift shop down the street. They even came and got it. You know the one—the sales support the homeless shelters."

"Do you see the irony in that?" Mrs. Moore frowned. "Homeless. You could be homeless."

"But I'm not, Mom. I will have a home, in North Dakota."

"Did you call, to see if it was available?"

"I'm waiting to hear."

Her mother sprang on the words, like a triumphant duck nabbing a fat beetle. "Waiting? Waiting for what? They haven't called you back?"

This was the problem with the visual part of this computer chat program. Her mother could see her expression, so Livvy faked a hearty smile. "It was an address."

"An address?"

Don't ask me any more questions, Livvy pleaded silently. If her mother found out it was a post office box number, she'd never hear the end of it.

"So how do you know—" Mrs. Moore began, but Livvy broke into the sentence.

"Mom, if this makes you feel better, I have enough in my savings to stay in a motel for months. I will not be homeless."

"So you're driving out there—you have your car insurance up to date?"

"Mom! I'm twenty-five years old! I know about car insurance."

Actually she had sold her car. It was good in the city, but it wasn't the kind of thing she'd want to drive across the country. Instead, in her purse right now were airplane tickets to North Dakota.

"Oh Livvy," her mother said, "you know your dad and I want the best for you, but we think you're being hasty. Please think this through."

"I know, Mom. I know."

"Be careful," her mother advised. "You know how we worry."

"I do."

Mercifully her mother's phone rang, and the conversation ended. Livvy turned off her computer and leaned back in her chair.

Had she convinced her mother that she was in control of this situation? More importantly, had she convinced herself?

It would have been so easy to stay in Boston, living this life that was split between two spots: behind her desk helping people fulfill their hearts' desires of a home, and in front of her television, vicariously dreaming of what was out in the world, just waiting for her, for someday. . . .

It was time to move away from the desk and the television, and to stretch, to explore, to find herself.

This may not have been the most conventional way, but it would work.

She had it all set up. Everything was ready. She just had to go.

❧

It was the one thing Livvy hadn't thought of when throwing things together for her hurried flight to North Dakota—how to get to Sunshine from the last airport.

She was so tired. The only flight—make that the only flights—she could get with such short notice had hippity-hopped her all over the southern and midwestern United States. She'd always wanted to travel, but this was ridiculous. She'd been to Charleston, Baton Rouge, Oklahoma City, Indianapolis, over to Kansas City, up to Detroit, to Minneapolis, then to Bismarck, and finally a puddle jumper had brought her here, to Obsidian. It was so tiny it didn't even have a dot on the map.

Or a car rental agency.

But thanks to a young lad at the airport, who saw an enterprising way to make some money, she was seated behind the wheel of a pickup truck, rattling her way toward Sunshine.

She turned on the radio and smiled. The teenager had some priorities. The truck had satellite radio.

She hit a bump and the book on the seat beside her slid onto the floor. She'd bought it in the Indianapolis airport—or maybe it was Detroit—and read it eagerly. *The Complete Guide to Home Construction and Repair.* She'd had some doubts about how thoroughly the topic could be covered in 249 pages, but it had been enlightening.

Something alongside the road moved, and she slowed to a stop. A family of deer watched her curiously, and she spoke to them from inside the truck. "You're wondering what I'm doing here, aren't you? Well, so am I."

She wasn't the kind of person to be impetuous, but here she was, on a gravel road in North Dakota. Just two weeks ago, she'd been sitting in traffic in Boston, reaching for that stray newspaper. If it hadn't blown up against her car, if she hadn't picked it up, if she hadn't been stuck in traffic, if she hadn't lost her temper with Mr. Evans. . . It was an amazing chain of sequences.

She got out of the truck and stretched. The deer took one last look at her and bounded away, and she was alone, except for the warbling melody of a bird.

Along the western horizon, jagged peaks sprouted up. The colors were wild. Russet and brick with terra cotta and cinnamon. The Badlands.

Beside their wonder, under a sky that was the purest blue she'd ever seen, she felt suddenly a part of it all. A tiny part, but a part nevertheless.

Praying hadn't been something she'd done a lot of lately, unless she counted urging God to let her car start on a cold morning, or pleading with Him to let there not be a long line at the drive-up coffee place.

Now though, when it was just her, the deer, and the Badlands, it became important to recognize God's handiwork and to put herself in His mighty hands.

"God, I don't know what I'm doing here, but I'm going to need some help. You've put me here for some reason, I'm sure, and I want to thank You for choosing such a spectacular setting." She paused. "Amen."

She got back into the truck, and after several noisy tries, got it to start.

This was an amazing trip. Here she was, Livvy Moore, in North Dakota, on a gravel road in a pickup truck with a gun rack in the back, headed for a place she'd been drawn to by the sheer appeal of a windblown ad.

Amazing.

❧

"Ready for a break?" Hayden stopped sorting through the

lumber pile and stood up, his back protesting vehemently.

"Yup." Gramps pulled his straw hat off, ran his hand over his nearly bald head, and stuck the hat back on again.

The two of them had tackled yet another outbuilding. This one held smaller pieces of wood, salvaged apparently from the old boathouse.

"Look, Gramps." Hayden handed him a sign that was in the heap. BUDDY SYSTEM SWIM—

"Remember that? You had the buddy system rule over at the swimming beach."

"Save it," his grandfather said, taking the sign and laying it aside. "We'll fix it and use it again."

"But there's no swimming beach anymore. Remember, Gramps?"

Gramps frowned a bit, and the veil came over his eyes that Hayden was seeing much too frequently. His grandfather got confused more and more, and details didn't stay with him.

Hayden put his arm around his grandfather's shoulders, trying to ignore the clutch of fear that assailed him whenever he felt how thin his grandfather had become. Under the red flannel shirt he could feel every angle of the old man's bones.

"Let's go inside and have a root beer," he said gently, guiding Gramps back to the house.

Once inside the cool kitchen, he uncapped two brown bottles of root beer. "Just like the old days, right, Gramps?" he asked as they took deep sips of the icy sweet drink. "Remember how we used to come into the canteen and buy root beer and those candy ropes? We'd eat them until we were sick."

Gramps laughed, his gaze bright and snappy again. "Everyone was covered with sand and the flies came in because you kids couldn't remember to shut the screen door."

"That screen door never shut anyway. Those were some good times, weren't they?"

"You know what was my favorite?" his grandfather asked. "The bonfire."

Hayden smiled, transported back to those summer evenings at the bonfire his grandfather built each night. The kids had their favorite marshmallow-roasting sticks, and dodging the sparks to get your marshmallow done perfectly was part of the fun. "Does anything taste better than a marshmallow cooked over a bonfire?" he asked. "So hot you can't eat it, and so gooey you can't help yourself. Of course, the best ones are the ones that catch fire and turn black. Yum!"

"And the vespers." Gramps leaned forward. "Remember the vespers?"

"Of course. Every bonfire ended with a prayer. It was the perfect ending to perfect days."

Gramps turned to him and wrapped his gnarled fingers around Hayden's hand. "Grub, we had good times here. But we can't keep Sunshine wrapped in a bubble. We've got to move on. You're a grown man now, teaching math, no less, to those high school kids. And me? I'm an old codger who gets his nows mixed up with his thens."

"You're doing fine, Gramps, and you're coming with me to live in Obsidian," Hayden reminded him. "You've got to make sure I don't do anything too goofy."

Gramps chuckled. "And vice versa."

A loud sound, like a gunshot report, broke the afternoon silence. "What was that?" Hayden asked, bounding out of his chair and reaching for the screen door.

A horn honked. And honked again. And again.

He tore out of the kitchen and across the yard. An old truck was parked there, with a woman trying to do something to the hood of it while the horn continued to honk.

"What are you doing?" he hollered at her.

"It won't stop!" she yelled back. "And I can't get this hood thing to open."

"There's a lever inside you pull first."

"I know." She held it up. "It came off in my hand."

Fortunately there was enough rust on the truck to make opening the hood fairly easy, and Hayden disconnected the horn.

"Sorry about that," the woman said, smiling at him. "And sorry about that bang. This thing backfires something fierce."

She reached her hand out to him. "I'm Livvy Moore, and I want to buy Sunshine."

two

The two men stared at her, and Livvy's smile began to fade.

"This is Sunshine, isn't it? I have the advertisement right here on the front seat." She pulled the door of the truck open, and had to slam it twice to make it latch. "Sorry," she added. "It's not mine. A young fellow rented it to me."

"It's Trevor's truck," the older man said. "Boy has a fool's heart but an accountant's mind."

"Excuse me?" The conversation had just started and she was already lost.

The younger man stepped forward. "I'm Hayden Greenwood and this is my grandfather, Charlie Greenwood. Please excuse our manners. We don't get many folks visiting."

"I'm not visiting," she said. "Unless Sunshine is already sold?"

Behind Haywood, his grandfather grinned. "Nope."

"Gramps and I were just sitting down to a root beer in the kitchen. Would you like to join us? We'll be more comfortable in there, out of the sun," Hayden said.

For a breath of a moment, Livvy paused. In Boston, she would never have gone into a house with two men she didn't know, but on the other hand, she wasn't in Boston. These guys didn't look dangerous, and if they were, her fate was sealed anyway. What was she going to do? Leap into the rattletrap pickup truck which might or might not start?

Clutching the advertisement in her hand, she nodded

and followed them. The house was a traditional two-storied home, plainly structured with no extra gingerbread features, slatted decorative shutters the only nod to adornment.

Why had she chosen open-toed shoes? The ground was a strange mixture of sand and tiny pebbles and loose red dirt, and it quickly worked its way inside her designer shoes where it ground away at the soles of her feet, and it certainly wasn't doing her hosiery any good either.

She hobbled behind the men, trying not to wince as the debris dug even deeper into her feet.

At the door of the house, she surreptitiously slipped her feet out of the open sandals and shook the soil and stones out, vowing never again to wear those torturous things here.

The inside of the house was welcoming. In the open windows, light yellow curtains lifted and billowed in the afternoon breeze. An old-fashioned oscillating fan whirred in the corner, keeping the air moving.

"This is such a comfortable home, Mr. Greenwood," she said as the older gentleman caught the screen door so it didn't slam behind them.

His face crinkled into a smile. "Do us all a favor and call me Gramps. You use city words like *Mr. Greenwood* here and nobody'll know who you mean. Right, Grub?"

"Grub?" she asked.

Hayden rubbed his grandfather's shoulder. "Only Gramps can call me Grub. The rest of the world is forced to call me Hayden."

She liked them already. The love between the two was clear.

She looked around the living room.

The floors were wooden—the original planks, she was

sure, judging from the soft satiny patina and the slight dip in the floor leading from the front door to the kitchen, the worn path of many feet heading for a treat or a cup of coffee after coming from the outside.

A large braided rug, its edges curled and mended, had also held its place of honor in the middle of the living room for at least two generations. She'd noticed similar ones at auctions in Boston, going for quite a fine price as what the decorators called "vintage Americana."

A tabby cat, the biggest one Livvy had ever seen, was curled in the middle of the rug. It opened one eye and looked at Livvy with a deep golden gaze and then, apparently deciding that the newcomer was no one important, shut the eye again and began to snore.

"That's the only cat left here. Got the last of the barn cats—or resort cats, most rightly—adopted out a week ago. No, this is Martha Washington," Gramps said with a fond smile at the slumbering cat.

"Martha Washington?" she asked.

"She came pre-named." Hayden knelt and stroked the cat's back, but the animal was clearly unimpressed, and slept on. "We inherited her from a lady in Obsidian who let her granddaughter name her. Why she chose that is a mystery that is unsolved today. And the goofy cat doesn't answer to anything else."

"Critter doesn't answer to anything," Gramps said, shaking his head. "She has a brain the size of a peach pit."

"Now, now," Hayden said with a chuckle. "You love that cat."

Gramps harrumphed. "By the way, Miss Moore, the cat comes with Sunshine. Don't want her? That's a deal-breaker."

"Call me Livvy, and the cat is welcome."

"No changing your mind," Gramps warned. "But let's get back to those root beers and see if we can cool ourselves off a bit."

She followed the men into the kitchen, which was bigger than the living room. Cabinets lined three of the four walls, with breaks only for two large windows. The fourth wall was covered with framed photographs, plaques with mottos and Bible verses engraved on them, and a painting of the Last Supper.

"Root beer?" Hayden asked as Gramps pulled out her chair for her.

The table and chairs were from the early 1950's. The chairs were upholstered in red vinyl, patched and re-patched with tape, and the tabletop was a matching marbleized red plastic with a dented aluminum edge that ran around it.

"Root beer would be lovely."

"Back in the good old days," Gramps said as he stared at a photo on the wall, "we had a big cooler that we kept all different kinds of pop in. Green River, Yoo-hoo, grape Nehi—remember those, Grub? Your favorite was Green River. Or was that your dad's?"

"Dad's," Hayden answered. "I was always a root beer fellow myself, just like you, Gramps."

"Root beer is mighty good," the older man said, "especially when you drink it out of a Sunshine glass."

"Right you are," Hayden said. "Coming right up."

Soon they were pouring root beer into tall blue glasses with SUNSHINE, NORTH DAKOTA, on the side.

"We used to have these by the boxful," Hayden said. "Now we're down to just a few."

"You'd better order some more, then," his grandfather said.

"We don't need them," Hayden reminded him. "Sunshine closed as a resort two years ago."

"End of an era, end of an era." The old man sighed.

"So," Hayden said, looking directly at her with eyes that were an amazing light blue, "you're considering buying Sunshine, Miss Moore?"

"It's Livvy, please. If you'll sell it to me, I'll buy it."

She heard her own voice speaking the words, but it all seemed like a dream. This was so out of character—but maybe she didn't know what her own character was, having had it buried under the heavy thumb of Michael Evans for too many years.

"Why?" Gramps's question was direct.

"Because I—" She faltered. How could she explain the series of circumstances that had led her there?

She looked at the two men sitting across from her, and began. When she had finished telling the story of the windblown paper, she said, "I think it was one of those God things. Do you know what I mean?"

In the Boston agency, with the people she usually dealt with, the answer would have been a benevolent chuckle, but here the reaction was different. After a moment, both men nodded. "We do know," Hayden said.

"God works in mysterious ways," Gramps added. "Very mysterious. Sometimes I wish I knew what He had planned for us, but this life is one long voyage to our reward. He's given us a map, and we can stay on the road and enjoy the ultimate destination, or we can do like most of us do and meander all over the countryside, taking wrong turns and finding dead ends."

"So you believe that God led you here," Hayden said.

She swallowed. It sounded as if they had lived their lives as Christians. It wasn't that she hadn't, but she had taken many of those wrong turns.

"Maybe," she said slowly, "it's about time I listened to Him."

Hayden leaned back in his chair and ran his fingers through his straw-colored hair, bleached by the summer sun. "Sunshine was always run by His principles, you see. One of our favorites is: 'Therefore all things whatsoever ye would that men should do to you, do ye even so to them.'"

"That's the Golden Rule, kind of," she said.

He laughed. "You're right—kind of. We have it right up here in its traditional format, the one everybody learns as a kid. The Golden Rule isn't just something we have on the wall." He pointed to one of the many plaques displayed beside them. "Those words are the foundation of everything we've done here for three generations."

"*Do unto others*," she said, and as she spoke the words, her stomach twisted. It was such a basic tenet of living—one she'd let herself forget.

"*As you would have others do unto you*," Hayden finished. "I know that in some businesses, the rest of the line is *Before they do unto you*, but that's not the way we operated."

"Our customers were family. Some still are, but the fact is that there's not money to be made in this any longer," Gramps added. "The big vacation spots have advertising budgets that we just couldn't compete with."

There was no rancor in his words. It was evident that he had come to peace with the fact that Sunshine wasn't what it had been in the past.

"What do you plan to do with Sunshine?" Hayden asked.

The question brought her up short. It was the one part of her plan—if she could call her half-baked, spur-of-the-moment decision a "plan"—that she hadn't developed completely.

"I'm not sure," she said. "I just know that I want to be here."

"Because God sent you here?" Gramps asked, and his eyes, the same sky blue as his grandson's, but clouded, met hers squarely.

She nodded. "Yes."

"Maybe," Hayden suggested, "you'd like to see Sunshine before you decide. Drain those root beers and let's go out for a walk."

She groaned inwardly at the thought of walking even one more step outside with her sandals on but she smiled and stood up. "I'm game."

As if reading her mind, Hayden asked, "Do you have some sneakers you could put on? Those shoes don't look very comfortable."

She started to shake her head but then she remembered that in the borrowed truck was her suitcase, and in that suitcase was a pair of rubber-soled shoes that she'd tucked in at the last minute, in case there was an exercise facility at Sunshine. She almost laughed at how clueless she'd been.

Soon, with her feet in the shoes that had cost her a week's pay, she began the tour of Sunshine.

"Here's an outbuilding," Hayden said, "and there's another one, and there's another one, and there's another one."

"What are they all for?" she asked.

"For storing lumber from torn-down sheds in case we want to build more." He grinned at his grandfather.

"This larger one was once the canteen," Gramps said, ignoring the good-natured gibe. "That's where kids used to come in from swimming and buy taffy and pop."

"And the parents would gather in the late afternoon or evening for a rousing game of Monopoly or Clue," said Hayden. "In the evening, we'd grill hamburgers and hot dogs or serve some of Gran's famous tater tot hot dish. On rainy days, which were rare but they did happen, everyone would gather there and we'd play charades."

"Now it's a storeroom." Gramps opened the door and led them inside.

Boxes were piled haphazardly around the perimeter of the room. On one end, a counter divided a small kitchen from the rest of the building. Dust motes danced in the midafternoon sun, and Livvy thought that if she stood still and listened hard enough, she'd be able to hear the laughter of the years of customers.

"We had some good times here," Gramps said, running his hand over the back of a chair draped with what seemed to be an old curtain. "Do you remember, Grub?"

"I do."

The two men were lost in memories, touching the doorknob, the windowsill, the scattering of tables. With the kitchen and the bathrooms, now marked LADS and LASSIES in an old-style block print, it was easy to see what it had been.

Livvy walked around the room, her real estate training clicking into place. The canteen was a mess right now, but it had possibilities. For what, she wasn't sure, but it was there.

"Let's show her the swimming hole," Hayden said, breaking the silence.

They left the canteen and reentered the bright afternoon.

"This is beautiful," she said, looking at the vista that was so incredible it was almost overwhelming.

The Badlands, touched with coppery tones, surrounded them. Overhead, only one stray cloud drifted lazily, the sole break in the endless blue sky. In the distance, a bird trilled, its melody gracing the air with a song.

They passed a cluster of cabins, each one painted a different color that had probably once been bright but had faded to a softly muted hue. Each one sported a worn sign declaring its rather prosaic name: the GREEN CABIN, the YELLOW CABIN, the RED CABIN, the BLUE CABIN, and so on. She counted quickly: There were eleven of them.

A chicken, startled from its hunt for bugs in the dirt, flapped off in a great display of wings and feathers and screeching squawks that shattered the afternoon stillness.

The path to the small swimming area had been permanently etched in the ground by countless feet making their way to the water.

Hayden provided the narrative as they followed those long-gone footsteps.

"It's part of Little Starling, the river that goes through here. It makes a little bend here, and with the help of a tractor, a dredge, and some good old-fashioned elbow grease, that became Sunshine's version of a lake. Today it probably wouldn't be legal, but the river's adapted to it, so it's all good."

Around a straggling set of trees, the glistening water was a surprise in the dry landscape.

The pier, now weathered to a soft gray, was missing some of the boards, and it leaned to one side. A lifeguard station was near the sandy beach, but it was missing most of the steps to the top. Only a foolhardy soul would attempt to climb it.

Algae-laced waves lapped at the shore, and in the stillness, Livvy could hear more birds and the faint sound of insects buzzing along the water's edge.

"It needs some work," Gramps said.

"The whole thing needs work," Hayden said. "I don't know, of course, what you plan to do here, but the fact is that except for Gramps and me and our friends, no one comes here. Sunshine hasn't had any customers for two years now."

It was such a difference from the hustle of Boston. There were no car horns honking. No radios blaring. No one talking.

Livvy stood motionless, letting the nothingness of it all overtake her. She felt tiny and yet part of all creation. The soft breeze lifted and dropped her hair around her cheeks and forehead.

And, as she listened to the sounds of God Himself—the soft splash of the waves, the trill of the birds, the hum of the insects—she fell in love.

"I want it."

The words hung in the air. She saw the exchange of a glance between the two men, felt their sadness, and knew in her heart that with those three words, she had sealed all of their fates.

"Let's go back to the house," Hayden said at last.

She reluctantly tore herself from the idyllic scene and followed Hayden and his grandfather back up the path, past the odd assortment of outbuildings, and to the house with the ancient pickup truck parked in front of it.

Martha Washington acknowledged their return with the

flick of an ear, but otherwise didn't stir as they walked through the living room and back into the kitchen.

"I don't suppose in Boston they do much business at the kitchen table," Hayden said as they sat at the red dinette set.

Livvy laughed. "Some. But you're right, usually I'd invite you to my office and we'd draw up the paperwork there."

"You're still interested? Even after seeing the rest of Sunshine?" His tanned forehead furrowed into a concerned frown.

"Especially after seeing the rest of it."

Gramps's fingers traced a groove in the tabletop. "This has been our life for many years. Decades, in fact. It's—" His voice broke, and Hayden covered his grandfather's hands as the old man gathered himself. "It's hard, letting this go into a stranger's possession. It was everything to Ellie and me. Now she's gone, and I'm going to lose Sunshine, too."

"Gramps—" Hayden began, but his grandfather shook off the interruption.

"I need to say this." He took a deep breath and exhaled. "I hope you understand that I want a few days to absorb this, to make sure that we're doing the right thing."

"It's our only choice," Hayden said gently. "We can't do this any longer. Not this way. We have to let it go."

Livvy fought back the tears that suddenly choked her. She'd arranged many sales of family homes, some of them foreclosures, and most of them had torn at her heart, but none of them had been as personal as this. She'd never been the buyer, the one who was taking the property.

She reminded herself that this was a business transaction. They would receive payment for it, and it would probably be enough to keep them solvent for years to come. It was their choice. They had put the property up for sale. They had done it. Not her. She was merely the one who had come to their aid.

So why did she feel so terrible?

"Gramps, tonight we will pray about it," Hayden said, and his grandfather nodded. Then the old man pushed his chair back and stood up.

"I'm very tired. I hope you'll excuse me, Livvy, but I need to lie down."

She nodded. "Of course."

Hayden's eyes followed his grandfather's steps as he left the room and went into the living room. Neither of them spoke as they listened to the man's heavy tread as he climbed the steps to the second floor.

"My grandfather means everything to me," Hayden said at last. "Everything. It's important to me that he is at ease about this. Before we make any agreements, I want to make sure he understands."

"Certainly."

"Plus I know you'd like to see the house, too." He glanced upstairs, as if he could see right through the ceiling and into what must have been his grandfather's room, judging from the footsteps that she could hear through the plaster. "That will have to wait until tomorrow."

"I understand."

They stood up, and together they left the kitchen. In the living room, Martha Washington had woken up and was following Gramps up the stairs.

"She's his cat. No matter what he says, she is his." Hayden watched the cat climb the steep staircase. "The other cats have been adopted out, so she's the only one left. Despite what he said earlier about her coming with the property,

Gramps won't let her go—he can't let her go."

Livvy didn't know what to say. The entire thing—the decision to quit her job, put everything she owned into storage, and come to a state she knew nothing about—was overwhelming. Intensifying it all was seeing the interaction of the two men as they bid good-bye to a family treasure.

At the front door, he pulled a baseball cap from the coat tree there and shoved it on his head as soon as they stepped outside. She smiled as she read the printed words over the bill: COOTER'S HARDWARE.

Outside, he paused to move a chicken from in front of the doorway. It flapped its wings and objected strenuously as he placed it onto the ground. "We've managed to get our animals down to Martha Washington, who is about as much a barn cat as I am, and this hen. I suppose you could technically call her free-range, but it's mainly because she refuses to listen to us and stay in the coop area."

As if understanding exactly what Hayden was saying, the chicken glared at him with her beady eyes, clucked, and strutted right back onto the porch.

Livvy and Hayden looked at each other and laughed. "See what I mean?" he asked. "Not only has she made this entire place her home, she has attitude. At least she does go back to the coop to lay her eggs, although once in a while this old lady"—he pretended to scowl at the recalcitrant chicken— "she'll think she's funny and plop an egg in a lawn chair, so you'd be wise to check before you sit down out here."

"It'll be hard for you to part with Sunshine, won't it?" she asked.

He turned his head and studied the horizon, with the irregularly shaped buttes notching into the sky. "This has been part of life since I was an infant," he said at last. "Oh, I was born in Bismarck, and I went to college in Grand Forks on one end of the state and Williston on the other, but Sunshine was where my heart was. My grandparents ran this place from the time they were married, and the highlight of every summer was coming here. And then when my parents died, Gramps and Gran took me in and I moved to Sunshine permanently."

"It's part of your family," she said softly.

He tugged the baseball cap off and ran his hand over the top of his head. The sun caught his golden hair for just a moment before he slapped it back on and moved off to shoo the chicken away again.

"It is. Gran died two years ago, and Gramps lost his heart. He decided to close Sunshine then. He said he couldn't have one without the other."

Livvy wished she had her sunglasses with her to hide her eyes, which were once again filling with tears.

"One day," Hayden said, "one day I want to have what they did."

"Sunshine, you mean?"

"I mean their love. They not only finished each other's sentences, they often spoke together. I remember being a kid and watching them sit next to each other. They breathed in unison. My mom used to say that their hearts beat as one. When Gran died, Gramps. . ."

His words trailed off, and she put her hand on his arm. "It must have been really difficult."

He nodded. "He's gotten vague and forgetful now. It's for the best that we sell Sunshine. I can stay with him in the summer, but I teach in Obsidian in the winter, and I can't always get out here to check on him. It's a trek in the winter as you might imagine. The road gets pretty nasty when the snow comes, and I worry about him. He can't drive anymore. And with our winters here, somebody can't always get to him."

"It's the sensible thing to do," she said.

"Sensible—but horrendously painful." He straightened his back. "Well, as we know, we can want what we want, but that doesn't mean we can have it. Meanwhile, do you have lodging in Obsidian?"

"I'm going to be staying at the Badlands Vista Motel."

He winced. "You'll want to move out of there rather quickly. Lu and Ev, the owners, are as honest as the day is long, but they haven't upgraded anything there in at least twenty years, and that includes the mattresses, I've heard. How long are you planning to stay?"

Livvy leaned against the side of the house and studied the man in front of her. He really was amazingly good-looking— his face was tanned, his eyes were an astonishing bright blue, and his legs were long and rangy in the denims he was wearing—but had something gone wrong with his brain?

Hadn't they just spent most of the afternoon discussing her buying the old resort?

"I am planning to stay here," she said, her voice sounding, to her relief, sure and strong.

"Here? Oh no. No. No, that won't work." He looked quite distressed.

"Well, not *here*. Not right away, that is. You and your grandfather will need some time to find a place to stay, and I don't know how long you'll need because I'm not familiar with the housing situation in Obsidian, if that's where. . .you'll be. . . staying?" Her words faded away as he began to laugh.

" 'Housing situation'? Obsidian has one apartment building, which is where I live in the winter. It's got four units and is nearly as bad as the Badlands Vista Motel, but not quite. It's cleaner, for one thing. I don't know what we'll do."

"I have no intention of kicking you out of your home. There are still many dotted lines to sign on—inspections and assessments, transfers and titles—before the deed changes hands." She knew from her experience working for Mr. Evans that one could never plan definitively on moving in quickly. There was almost always some snag somewhere. Paperwork didn't arrive on time, floodplain issues appeared, a banker was on vacation—they'd all happened.

"This is really sudden," he said. "I have to say that when Gramps and I put the advertisement in the *Bismarck Tribune*, we never thought it would travel all the way to Boston, and certainly we hadn't even dreamed that someone would take us up on it. If you don't mind, I'd like to take a little time to consider this."

She clutched the edge of the railing that ran around the porch. He couldn't back out of it. The tumbledown resort, with its crazy assortment of colorful sheds and the rainbow of cabins and the dusty canteen, had taken root in her heart.

"We have no choice except to sell," Hayden continued, his voice so quiet that it seemed as if he were talking to himself. "We have no choice."

"I don't want to rush you, but—" She stopped before saying what was obvious to both of them, that he and his grandfather needed to sell, and she was a ready buyer. In any market, a decrepit, closed-down resort in the middle of nowhere would attract few buyers, and in this market, anyone showing even a faint glimmer of interest needed to be kept close to the deal.

He pulled the cap from his head and once again smoothed his hair and shoved the cap back on. "Tomorrow let's get you set up with a decent place to stay. I think this will all work out. If it's His will, it's my will."

She nodded. "I'll see you in the morning, then. Here? Or in Obsidian?"

"Meet me at Clara's Café, at eight?"

"I'll see you then."

She climbed back into the truck Trevor had rented to her, and she was aware that Hayden was watching her as she tried several times to start it. Just when she thought she'd certainly flooded the engine, it caught in a great blaze of muffler sounds and backfires, and she waved as she pulled away from the resort and onto the county road to Obsidian.

So this was Sunshine.

Her mind was spinning with the possibilities of what could happen with it. Given the proper amount of love and care, it could come to life again. She was sure of it.

An idea had started to take root. Maybe it wasn't possible, but maybe it was.

The vision of those little shacks scattered around the house poked at her mind, begging for her to pay attention to them. Could she do it?

Fishing.

Hayden hadn't mentioned it during the tour, but the advertisement had touted it. If the fishing was good, then maybe, just maybe, it would work.

The idea wandered around in her brain, picking up momentum as she began to see the possibilities.

A fishing resort. People loved to fish. On the Travel

Channel, she'd seen shows about folks going deep-sea fishing to get marlins or some other huge fish. Of course, there wasn't a deep sea around here, but there had to be something swimming in that river.

It was good. It was. It would take a lot of work, but she wasn't above that. If she did most of it herself, it wouldn't cost a horrendous amount.

She'd never swung a hammer but just the thought of it sounded wonderful. Nailing boards into place, putting up drywall, even plumbing. None of it was too much for her.

Yes, she was headed into the construction business. She patted the book beside her. *The Complete Guide to Home Construction and Repair.* It would be her Bible.

Her Bible.

She remembered the faith she'd seen displayed. Hayden and Gramps hadn't said much, but their belief was clearly the cornerstone of their existence.

She'd gone to Sunday school and church when she was young, in the little town on the western edge of Massachusetts, but when she got to be a teenager, overnights and weekend getaways with her friends had taken precedence, and she'd never gotten back to it.

She pulled at last into the motel parking lot, and let herself into her room. She picked up the remote control for the television and clicked it, but nothing happened. The batteries were probably dead.

It was all right. She wasn't in the mood for watching television anyway. Instead, she sprawled across the bed, the pillows bunched under her, and opened her laptop. The motel, as old and decrepit as it was, managed to have a fairly good wireless signal, and soon she was connected with her mother.

"Hey, Mom. It's Livvy. You'll never guess where I am."

"Livvy! Are you all right? What happened? You're in North Dakota? What's it like?"

"It's incredible. It's just incredible. I don't know any other way to say it. It's incredible."

"And what's this place like? The place you want to buy?"

"Sunshine is incredible. The owners are incredible. Mom, am I saying *incredible* enough?"

Her mother laughed. "I'm just guessing, but I gather the place is incredible? I'd love to see it, and I wish your dad and I could get there to help you, but we're stuck here until December. I'm sorry, hon. I feel bad, but we're tied up with our teaching."

"I understand, Mom," she said.

"You're not in over your head, are you?" her mother asked, suddenly serious. "This isn't really like you. Usually you're such a quiet young woman. I expected you to be working for Mr. Evans forever."

"That's just it," Livvy said, noticing a water stain on the ceiling over the foot of the bed. Luckily it looked old. "I needed a change."

"There's a boy, isn't there?"

"A boy? Mom, I'm twenty-five years old!"

"Okay, a man. A young man. There's a young man involved with this, isn't there?"

Livvy thought of Hayden as he stood on the porch, his gaze fixed on the Badlands silhouetted against the sky, his hair as golden as reflected sun, and the tenderness in his voice as he talked about his grandfather.

She changed the subject. With mothers, it was the safest thing to do when young men were involved.

Hayden sat on the porch, ignoring the chicken that pecked at his shoestring. This day, which had started out dealing with the endless supply of boards, had moved into the promise of fishing, and then ended with a flourish when Livvy Moore had driven up in Trevor's truck, which had more filler than original metal.

He shook his head. That truck—he'd have to have a talk with the young Trevor about putting a city woman into it and then sending her out on the county roads, some of which were so washboarded that you risked your teeth driving on them, you'd be so jarred by the unevenness. If the truck had broken down, what would she have done?

She probably had a fancy cell phone, but coverage was spotty out here, and only one company provided any service. If she wasn't with that provider, the only thing her phone would be good for was—well, he couldn't think of anything it would be good for.

He sat forward suddenly, startling the chicken so much that it squawked at him and flapped off to sit on the railing and watch him with a wary eye.

What bothered him, what he needed to know for once and for all, was why she was there, wanting to buy Sunshine.

She had told them the story of the windblown newspaper and he had no reason to doubt its veracity. But there were many unanswered questions. What was a Bismarck newspaper doing in Boston? Why did it blow up against Livvy's car? Why hers?

He stared at the chicken, which walked sideways along the railing while clucking to itself.

"Do you have any ideas, chicken?"

Apparently it didn't, for with a flap of wings, it propelled itself from its perch to the seat of the chaise longue on the other end of the porch.

"Don't even think about laying an egg there," he warned, but the chicken settled in, still keeping watch on him. He'd have to check the crease in the cushion later in the day.

The front door swung open, and his grandfather came out and joined him on the porch.

"I couldn't sleep," Gramps said. "Kept thinking about this whole thing, and then I thought Ellie was making a peach pie. It sure smelled good."

Hayden patted his grandfather's hand. He didn't trust himself to speak.

Gramps continued, "But then I remembered that she was gone, and you know, I guess maybe I was asleep and just dreaming, wasn't I?"

"Maybe."

"When you were just a little pup, Grub, you came to your grandmother and me and asked how we knew that this life wasn't just a dream."

"And what did you say?" Hayden knew the answer, but he loved to hear the story.

"I did what any sensible grandfather would have done. I yelled, 'Wake up!' at you as loud as I could."

Hayden laughed. "You nearly scared me into the next year!"

Gramps shrugged. "Made my point. If that didn't wake you up, it wasn't a dream."

Hayden let the afternoon breeze drift over him as he sat next to his grandfather. How often he had taken these moments for granted, but now each second seemed precious, measured as it was.

He was not only losing Sunshine, he was losing his grandfather.

A scratching at the door broke into his train of thought. He got up and let Martha Washington out. She waddled over to Gramps's feet, and he scooped her up and placed her in his lap.

She stretched out, draping herself across his thin and bent legs, and shoved her head under his hand so he would pet her. Her purr filled the air, and Hayden shut his eyes.

He wanted to savor this moment, a time of perfection, a—

It all happened at once. The cat screeched and tore across his arms and knees, claws out, while the chicken attacked it with beak and talons. Hayden reached into the skirmish and separated the two.

He got the chicken off the porch and the cat back into the house before rolling his eyes at his grandfather.

"Wow, that fray was a furious flapping and flurry of feathers," Gramps said with a twinkle in his eyes. "Hey, maybe I've got a second career as a poet!"

Hayden shook his head. "As they say in the movies, don't quit your day job, Gramps. Don't quit your day job."

"My day job, huh? You are a hoot and a half, Grub. My day job is making sure Martha Washington doesn't take out the chicken."

"Or that the chicken doesn't take out Martha Washington."

They settled back and looked out at the vast panorama.

"This is the end of it," Gramps said.

"Maybe. It's your call." Hayden glanced at his grandfather. "I don't want you to make a decision you're not comfortable with."

"I think she'll be all right, don't you?"

"Who? Gran?" Hayden's stomach twisted, as it always did when Gramps's mind slipped.

"No, you goof. Livvy."

"She doesn't have a clue what to do with it," Hayden said.

Gramps laughed. "You'll be here to advise her."

"Once Sunshine is hers, I won't have anything to say about it."

"Sure," his grandfather said. "Sure. You go ahead and think that."

Hayden thought of Livvy, the way her short dark hair was tossed in the gentle summer breeze as she stood by the swimming hole, her dark eyes, deep with sympathy, watching his grandfather. She was going to be good for Sunshine.

three

Livvy stood in front of the mirror that was attached to the wall of the old motel. She brushed and rebrushed her hair, but no matter what she tried, it wouldn't lay flat. An early morning rain threatened, and her hair responded as it always did in high humidity. It became a dark brown curly mop.

Someone knocked at her door. It was probably the maid coming to straighten the room.

"Just a second," she called. "I'll be out in a minute."

"I can wait," a male voice answered, "although it's starting to sprinkle."

Hayden!

She gave her hair one last desperate swipe with the brush and shook her head in despair. It was not going to cooperate.

"I'm coming now."

She slipped on a zippered sweatshirt, pulled the hood over her wayward hair, and stepped outside.

He was hunched against the light sprinkle, his ever-present Cooter's Hardware cap on his head. "Ready for one of Clara's omelet specials?"

"I was going to meet you there, but I'm glad for the company on the walk over." She looked at the sky, which was dark with clouds. By the end of the day, she'd look like she had a small poodle sitting on her head. She pulled the string on her hoodie tighter.

"I've got an umbrella in the car, not that it does us any

good in there," Hayden said, grinning through the mist. "Do you have one?"

"Somewhere. That's the problem with moving. Everything is somewhere, but I have no idea where it is. It might be at my old office in Boston, still hanging on the back of the door. Or in the storage unit with my couch. Or on its way here now, courtesy of We Really Move You."

"We Really Move You?" he repeated.

"It's a relocation service I used, consisting of three college students and a herd of old vans."

"Vans don't come in herds."

She laughed. "You couldn't look at this group of vehicles and call them a 'fleet,' not by any stretch of the imagination."

"I see," he said, grinning back at her. "You know, the café is about half a block away. Should we brave it? We should be fine, unless the skies follow through on their threat and completely open up."

"Let's go for it."

"Gran used to say that God made us washable so we'd go for walks in the rain. Gramps wasn't convinced."

"I can imagine."

They hurried through the light rain. A large pickup truck was parked in front of the café, and in the back of the cab, she could see a rifle rack.

This definitely wasn't Boston.

The warm aroma of bacon and toast and coffee and something lusciously cinnamon-scented drifted toward them as they approached the building with the sign swinging overhead, proclaiming that Clara's Café was the home of the best omelet in the Dakotas.

"Is that true?" she asked, pointing at the sign.

"Absolutely. Trust me on that," he said solemnly.

As soon as they stepped inside, Hayden took off his cap and ran his fingers through his hair.

Guys had it so good, she thought. That was all it took. They didn't even need an actual comb, just their fingers. Whereas she'd struggled with a comb, a brush, an electric straightener, gel, and spray, and she knew that as soon as she let the hood fall, that effort would be for naught.

Well, she might as well get it over with. She untied the string and with a quick shake of her head, let the hood drop.

"Hey!" he said, looking at her hair, which she could feel springing out in all directions even as she stood there. "I like your hair like that!"

"You do?" She couldn't resist reaching up and touching it to see how bad the damage was. It was worse than she'd thought. What didn't wave was curled, and what didn't curl was frizzed.

"You look real."

"Real what?" she asked cautiously.

A flush began at the base of his neck and climbed steadily to his face. "Real. Just real."

She was prevented from inquiring further by the arrival of a very tall, very thin woman who greeted Hayden with enthusiasm, flinging her arms around the man with abandon.

"This," he said to Livvy as soon as he was released from the pink cotton embrace, "is Clara herself. Clara, this is Livvy Moore."

"Glad to meet you," Clara said, grasping Livvy's hand and pumping it up and down as if it were the handle on a well. "Glad to meet you indeed! And honored to have you here today. Hayden, why don't you and your young lady sit right here?"

She led them to the corner table. "Sit here, and then you two little birdies can have all the privacy your little hearts desire!" Her gaunt hands flapped together happily. "I'll be right back with coffee."

Livvy knew that now she was the one who was blushing. She slid into the seat and picked up the menu that was leaned against the napkin holder.

"I'm sorry about that," Hayden said in an undertone. "Clara is, in Gramps's words, a frustrated Noah."

Livvy let the menu drop. "A frustrated Noah? What? She wants to build an ark?"

"No," he answered, laughing. "She wants everything living to be matched. She can't stand to see a guy without a girl."

"And that's the way it should be," Clara said, reappearing and pouring coffee into their cups. "By the way, I assume you want some of this, miss, but if you don't, the java hound you're with will finish it for you. And ignore his fresh mouth."

"Fresh mouth?" Livvy said, trying very hard not to snicker.

"Yes. Making fun of me. The natural order of things is in twos, that's my theory. Salt and pepper. Bacon and eggs. Steak and potatoes." Clara crossed her bony arms across her equally bony chest and glared at Hayden, but her lips twitched in what Livvy suspected was a suppressed smile.

"Miss Moore is here on business." Hayden's voice was serious but his eyes twinkled.

"There's business and then there's business," Clara shot back. "And speaking of business, I have one to tend to. You ready to order?"

"Clara, we just sat down. Give us a few, okay?"

As the woman turned and walked away, Livvy heard her mutter, "All this and I'll bet he orders the usual."

Hayden leaned across the table and said, in a conspiratorial whisper, "The sad thing is that she's right."

"What is the usual?" Livvy asked, glad to have the conversation on food rather than Clara's notion of pairing them up.

"An omelet, naturally, made with tomatoes and cheese. Hash browns and bacon, both extra crispy. Four slices of white toast with grape jelly. And, of course, coffee, without which I might very well cease to function."

With those words, he lifted his coffee cup in a mock salute and took a clearly grateful swallow. "Ah. Nobody, but nobody, can make coffee like Clara."

She took a sip and sighed. "This is truly extraordinary. She'd have people lining up for this in Boston."

Almost wraithlike, Clara appeared at their table again. "Did you have time to decide? The usual, right, Hayden? And for your lady?"

"I'm not his lady," Livvy objected, "and I'll have the same as Hayden."

"Sure. Whatever." Clara swept the menu from in front of Livvy and slid it back into place over the napkin holder.

Desperate to move the conversation in a different direction, Livvy broached the subject of the coffee. "What's your secret of this great coffee, Clara?"

"Waste not, want not."

"Excuse me?" Either Clara had misunderstood her, or vice versa.

"Waste not, want not," the woman repeated.

"Certainly." Livvy shot Hayden a "*Do you have any idea what she's talking about?*" look. Perhaps Clara was having moments of disconnecting from reality?

"How many eggs do you suppose I go through here every morning?" Clara asked, her dark eyes fixed on Livvy while her thin, lipstick-less mouth twisted in a wry smile.

"I have no idea." Livvy shrugged. "A couple dozen?"

Clara laughed. "A couple hundred is more like it. And I'll give you a hint that you can carry on into your household when you get married." She rolled her eyes in Hayden's direction, and Livvy sighed mentally.

"What is that?" Livvy asked, avoiding looking at Hayden.

Clara leaned in so close that Livvy could smell the woman's lily of the valley perfume over the scent of the griddle that permeated the entire café. "Eggs," she said in a stage whisper. "Eggshells, to be exact. You put those in your pot with the coffee grounds and whoo-ee, your java will taste like liquid gold."

Livvy smiled. She wasn't sure she wanted her coffee to taste like gold, but she understood the idea. "I've heard of that. Cowboys did that, right?"

Clara cackled. "I guess. In the big city, everybody only want lattes and cappuccinos. Here, though, you get coffee. Good coffee. No need for that fancy-schmancy stuff with the hoity-toity syrups and such. 'With whip,' I had a fellow say the other day. 'You want a whip?' I asked him. 'Why? You going to be the ringleader in a circus?'"

Hayden shook his head. "Clara, you are something else."

"Well," she said, lifting her chin proudly, "I'd rather be something else than just like everybody. Omelets are almost ready, by the way."

"But we just ordered—" Livvy began, and then stopped. "Ohhhh."

"Yup," Clara said, "had them going as soon as I saw young

Hayden step in the door. Boy never varies. He's been eating the same thing since he was a sprig of a boy. Somehow I didn't think today would be the day he'd switch to something as exotic as French toast."

Within minutes, Clara was at their table, a large platter heaped with food in each hand. "Eat up and be healthy!"

"Be healthy?" Livvy said, looking at the mound in front of her. It was a display of artery-clogging delight. And it smelled delicious.

"Before we begin, may I ask the blessing?" Hayden said.

"Blessing? Oh, grace. Definitely."

This wasn't something she had seen in her day-to-day life in the city, but then most of her lunches had been a granola bar and a cup of coffee from the dispenser in the building and had been consumed at her desk over paperwork.

Some people, she knew, held hands while they prayed, but Hayden just lowered his head and shut his eyes. She followed suit as he prayed, simply, "Lord, bless this food. Touch all of our actions with Your grace. We ask this in Your holy name. Amen."

She was surprised at how good the short prayer made her feel. It was refreshing.

"You ready to have the best of the best?" Hayden asked. "Dig in!"

Livvy took his advice and as soon as the first bite of omelet hit her tongue, she knew that the advertising was well-deserved. The outside was just crispy enough, and inside, the omelet was fluffy and light. It truly was the best she'd ever had.

As she ate, the sheer incongruity of the situation she was in struck her. Here she was, sitting in a café in North Dakota, unemployed, with a man she'd just met across from her, and she was planning on investing her life savings in a resort that had been closed for two years—a resort in the middle of the Badlands.

She must be insane. That was the only answer. Or dreaming. What was she planning to do with it? At some point she would have to earn a living—and how would she do that?

Fishing, of course, came to mind, but the fact was that she knew nothing about it—or running a resort—or what a fishing resort did in the winter, although she had once seen a program on the Travel Channel about ice fishing. That show constituted the sum total of her knowledge about ice fishing, hardly enough of a foundation to build a successful business on.

But she could learn of course. Everybody had to learn at some time. Nobody was born knowing this stuff. The trick was looking like you had though.

This was all so out of character for her. She was a nice, normal young woman with a nice, normal job in Boston. Or she had been until she'd taken total leave of her senses and come to North Dakota.

There was still time to change her mind. Nothing had been signed. She could still back out. Maybe she couldn't get her job back from Mr. Evans—although with the appropriate amount of groveling, he'd probably hire her again—but it wasn't too late to undo everything.

But this just didn't feel like a misstep. It felt right.

She took another bite of the incredible omelet. It was the best she'd ever tasted, even if it did come served with a side of Clara's quirkiness.

"Gramps and I talked more last night," Hayden said. He

nabbed a last bite of shredded potatoes and popped it into his mouth.

Livvy froze, her own fork stopped midway to her lips. This was what she had been waiting for. She leaned forward a bit, knowing that what he was about to say would tell her the direction her life would take.

These were her crossroads. The next words that Hayden uttered would change her life.

"If I wouldn't end up broke and the size of a barn, I'd eat Clara's breakfasts for every meal."

Her fork clattered to the plate. "Excuse me?"

"Good food." He wiped his mouth with a paper napkin.

"It is, but you said you and your grandfather talked last night? About selling Sunshine to me, I gather?"

"Yes, we did." He pushed the plate aside and leaned forward. "We're interested, to the point of saying yes, I might add, but we have a couple of questions we'd like answered."

"Shoot," she said, and then, remembering the truck they'd walked past with the rack in the back of the cab, doubled back on what she'd said. "Don't shoot. Just ask."

He grinned. "Okay, I won't shoot. But here are the questions." He reached into his shirt pocket and pulled out a list. "First, Gramps wants to know if you can keep the place from going back to nature."

"Back to nature?"

"Any building left unattended will eventually be reclaimed by nature. The wood will fall apart, and animals will move in. Once they're in there, it's nearly impossible to get the building back to its former glory."

"I won't let that happen."

He looked at her squarely. "How will you prevent that?"

"I'm going to live there."

As soon as the words were out of her mouth, a great peace descended on her. It was right.

"Alone?" he asked.

"Possibly. Probably. At the moment, yes."

"You're a woman."

"And you're observant."

"The Badlands can be aptly named, you know." A slight frown creased his tanned forehead.

"Listen," she said, suddenly a bit angry, "Boston has its moments, too. Every place does. I think I can handle it."

"Do you have a gun?"

She thought again of the truck with the rifle rack outside the café. "No, I don't, and I never will."

"How will you protect yourself?"

She shook her head. This was not going at all well. "I will protect myself by being careful and using the brains God gave me. I have never been in the practice of putting myself in bad situations, and it's usually served me well."

He nodded, his gaze never leaving her face. "That's good. But what if you find yourself staring down a rattlesnake?"

"A rattlesnake." She shrugged with an assurance she didn't feel. A rattlesnake had never been part of her plan. "The chances that I'd have a loaded gun at my fingertips and that I'd know how to use it without blasting off my own foot are pretty minimal—no, they're nonexistent. So I guess I'd have to say I would stand still and wait for him to go away on his own."

"That's the right answer."

"It's the only answer. Trust me, Hayden, if I went into the kitchen to get coffee one morning and there was a snake in there, I would be paralyzed with fright. I'd have no choice but to stand stock-still."

"You wouldn't have a rattlesnake in your house anyway. They'd be in the outbuildings and in the rocky parts on the edge of the grounds. They don't want to see you any more than you want to see them. Now, if you were a plump rabbit, that would be different."

"Ah. So I should probably ditch the fuzzy bunny slippers just in case, huh? It would be just my luck that I'd see Mr. Snake and he'd think I was wearing breakfast on my feet."

Hayden laughed. "Fuzzy bunny slippers? That's quite the image."

She pretended to fluff her hair. "We Bostonians are all about fashion. But back to the question. I see this as a challenge, one that I'm willing to take on. I've never backed down before when confronted with something that makes me work a little harder, learn a little more, dig a little deeper."

"Do you know anything at all about buildings?"

"I was in real estate management in Boston for several years. Actually, I was until a couple of weeks ago."

"Did you ever hammer a nail?"

She had to think fast. She'd hammered her fingernail one time with a can when she was trying to fix the edge of a countertop that had worked loose, but that was too far from the truth. She'd hung pictures, but that wasn't really hammering and they weren't really nails but tiny tacks. The heel of her shoe that was coming undone, the top of a can of touch-up paint for her apartment, the cabinet door that wouldn't quite close—she'd smacked a lot of things into place in her life, but hammering a nail?

"Not really. I mean, maybe years ago—but how hard can it be? You hit the nail with the hammer."

"I see. And have you ever used a saw?"

"No."

"A level?"

"No."

"A screwdriver?"

"Yes! I have!" She felt ridiculously happy about this. Finally, he mentioned a tool that she had used.

"What did you do with it?"

"I fixed my sunglasses. And my laptop. The little screw that holds the monitor on was coming out and I tightened it."

This was not coming out at all as she planned. She took a quick moment and regrouped her thoughts, drawing on the skills she'd learned from Mr. Evans. She could almost hear his voice: *"Never play defense. Always have the right of way. Steer the ship."*

He'd been quite the fellow for folksy adages, but he'd made her an effective agent for closing deals.

And his advice was apropos here. She took control of the conversation.

"I have years of experience in real estate. I know buildings. I know construction, even if I haven't done it myself. I know what has to be union-labor, and what can be done by handymen—or handywomen. The best contractor doesn't do it all. He or she knows when to call in help. And let's face it, Hayden—" She used a trick she'd employed many times in getting an unsure client to agree with her. She got closer, and dropped her voice. "All construction workers had to get in at the ground floor, no pun intended. Everybody starts somewhere."

"But they had skilled people training them. Who will train you?" Hayden asked. His logical query poked an immediate hole in her argument.

"I have resources to help me when I need help." It was true. . .sort of.

"Oh." He sagged in obvious relief. "You've got a crew?"

"I have resources," she repeated, although she could count them on two fingers of one hand: the book and the Internet.

"Super," he said, "because if you're relying on the Internet, good luck to you. There's no signal out at Sunshine."

No Internet. She tried not to choke.

"So the next question Gramps and I came up with," he said, referring to his list again, "is if you intend to live there while the remodeling is being done."

That one was easy.

"Yes."

"How soon do you need to move in?" he asked.

"As soon as possible, of course, but I know that you and your grandfather need some time to move out and get settled."

"I have a place here in town, and I'd be happy to have Gramps with me, but he says he won't."

"He's too independent, I gather?"

"That's part of it. He doesn't want to be a bother, that's what he says." Hayden stared sadly into his nearly empty coffee cup. "As if he could ever be a bother."

"One set of my grandparents lives in Arizona, and the other one lives in Maine." She chuckled. "My parents are always trying to get them to move closer to me, and I'd love it, too, but they have absolutely no interest in it."

"I would like Gramps to be close though. I'm hoping I can get him in at the senior living apartments, but you can guess what he says. 'They're for old people!'"

"I understand the need to get him settled, that it's a priority," she said. "Did you say you can help me find a place to live in Obsidian? Oh, wait. That's a lot to ask of you, since you need to deal with moving your grandpa, too."

"Actually, yours is easy. I hope you don't mind, but I think I have a place for you. This morning I dropped off some eggs—yes, we have the world's orneriest chicken but she does lay eggs, even if you do have to find where they left them—at Jeannie Baldwin's house, and got to talking with her. She said she had turned the garage into a guesthouse for her cousin, who, in Jeannie's words, 'up and married some fellow' and now wasn't going to use it. She's fretting because she spent a lot of money fixing it up."

"Maybe I could rent it!"

"You could. Knowing Jeannie, it'll be sparkling clean. The only thing that might be an issue is that she's taking off soon to go to Africa on a mission tour so you'd also have to watch her house."

"I can do that!" This was working out wonderfully, and a rush of relief coursed through her.

"And her dog. And her bird. And her fish. And her crab. The rabbit escaped or else you'd have to watch it, too."

"That's quite the menagerie," she said.

"It's a zoo, that's what it is. The only thing missing is a monkey and a zebra, and that's only because she hasn't thought of them yet, I'm sure." Hayden shook his head.

"She must like animals."

"That, my friend, is an understatement. I think we can get the bird and the fish moved to the church. I'm not sure about the crab. It's one of those that live in a painted shell. She saw it at a mall, at one of those kiosks, and felt sorry for it. So she bought it and carted it all the way back here to Obsidian."

Jeannie Baldwin was sounding like a fascinating woman.

"What kind of dog is it?"

He didn't answer at first. Then he said, slowly, "I have no idea. It's big. It's got a lot of fur and a lot of drool."

"It's friendly, right?" she asked, cautious about this beast. She had about as much experience with dogs as she did with hammers.

"Friendly? Oh yes. Friendly. Very friendly. He doesn't bite. The worst he would do is lick his enemy's face off, or maybe drown him in drool. But he will like you."

"And after six weeks, he goes back to Jeannie, and I go to Sunshine, right?" She ran the calendar in her head. Based upon her experience in the projects she'd managed in Boston, six weeks should be plenty of time.

Plus, as she had seen countless times on her favorite television shows about flipping houses—buying them, rapidly remodeling them, and selling them for a profit—six weeks would give her lots of wiggle room.

Fixing up Sunshine should take three weeks, tops, once she got in there and could work in a fairly empty place. She knew that much from the house remodeling programs she'd watched on television. The key was to have the place free of furniture and carpet, so time wouldn't be wasted cleaning during the renovation, but instead could be done in one great swoop—or sweep—at the end.

"Are there other questions on your list?" she asked.

"Just one. What are you going to do with Sunshine?"

The world, which had been spinning so merrily, came to a dead halt.

This was the one part of her plan she hadn't figured out,

and it was the most important part. Without it, this was a journey without a destination.

She quickly weighed her options of how to respond to the question.

She could lie and come up with some scenario of investors and plans. That wasn't going to happen. Lying was never a good idea. It might get you past an immediate situation, but it had been her experience that lies had longer legs and greater staying power than she did, and they always caught up with her.

Plus she couldn't lie to Hayden and Gramps, even if she knew she'd never get tripped up on her own words. They were honest people. She could not imagine either of them telling a lie.

They deserved what she knew—and what she didn't know.

"Well," she hedged, "I haven't decided yet if I will do anything more than live there, at least for the time being. I was thinking about a fishing resort."

He shook his head. "I'm afraid that probably won't work. Folks here don't go to a resort anymore to fish. They've got their own boats."

"Whatever I do, I can assure you that I won't turn it into anything that would bring embarrassment to you or your grandfather. It won't be a bar or anything like that."

"There's not a lot you can do with that property," Hayden warned. "It's too far away from the interstate to be commercially appealing."

"So you're saying I can't make it into a discount mall?" she asked. "Or a twenty-plex movie theater? Or a fireworks warehouse?"

The horrified look on his face let her know that he didn't

understand she was kidding, and she backtracked quickly. "I was just kidding. Just kidding!"

"Fireworks! You had me going there for a moment. At any rate, I think it'll all work out for both of us. How soon do you want to do this? Do you need more time to think?"

She probably did, but she didn't dare let herself think any more. She might talk herself out of it.

"No," she said. "No, I don't."

With those words, she felt as if she'd walked to the edge of a cliff—and taken one more step. She hadn't seen all of the house, she hadn't had an appraisal done on it, she hadn't looked at a plat map—she hadn't done anything she should have done.

"All right then. I'll talk to the real estate agent later today and get things started. Meanwhile, let's go look at Jeannie's guest house."

Clara waved them on past regarding the bill. "I'll put it on Charlie's tab. Tell the old coot to come in and see me sometime. I'll make him a Charlie special."

"A Charlie special?" Livvy asked as they left the café.

"My grandfather invented it, or so he claims. Scrambled eggs, loaded with onions, garlic, jalapeños, and sausage. I make him stay on the other side of the house for twenty-four hours after he eats one. Those things are lethal."

The sun had come out, and the morning mist was drying quickly. "Good fishing weather," Hayden said.

"Really? That's one thing I've never done."

"Do you want to learn?" he asked, apparently not bothered that just moments before she had been planning to embark on a career dependent on fishing.

"I should if I'm going to be living at Sunshine, I suppose. Does it involve worms?"

"Not necessarily."

She shrugged and smiled. "Then let's do it. Can we see Jeannie's guest house and also the real estate agent this morning? They're not far away, are they?"

"Livvy, we're in Obsidian, not Boston. Nothing is far away. Jeannie's place is right up the block, and the real estate agent is next to the Badlands Vista Motel."

Jeannie was in her backyard at the clothesline, a basket of laundry at her feet. Her mouth was full of clothespins, and she stuck them on the sheet she was hanging up.

"I'm so glad the sun came out," she said, "or I'd have had wet sheets draped across my living room like some house of horrors."

Hayden laughed. "You could never have a house of horrors, Jeannie. This, by the way, is Livvy Moore. She's going to buy Sunshine."

Livvy immediately liked Jeannie. A mop of reddish-gold curls topped the middle-aged woman's head, and her ready grin took Livvy in as if they were old friends.

"I'm glad to hear that! It's a great place and we have wonderful memories, but it's time to let someone else have at it and begin their own," Jeannie said. "I just don't want to see Charlie out there one more winter alone. I know you go out and see him, Hayden, but he really needs to be in town."

"I agree," Hayden said. "It's still going to be difficult."

Jeannie straightened one edge of the sheet she'd just hung on the line. "After church last week, you'd gone to get some coffee, and I found him headed out toward the street. Now, he's not a two-year-old who has been warned about going into traffic—and I guess we all know that there really isn't anything like traffic here anyway—but what worried me was

I asked him where he was headed, and he said he had to get the mail."

"The mail?" Hayden asked, clearly at a loss. "What did he mean by that? It's delivered to Sunshine."

"That's what I asked," she said, "and he stopped for a moment, shook his head, and turned and went back into the church."

The pain on his face was clear. "It's the right thing," he said almost to himself. "It's the right thing."

"Well, let's see about getting you out of that nasty Badlands Vista Motel and into a more comfortable place. Hayden tells me you're from Boston—"

Jeannie's chatter covered the sadness of the moment with a layer of cheer as the three headed over to the guesthouse.

The garage door had been removed and the wall replaced so expertly that Livvy, even with her expertise in the housing world, couldn't tell that this had once been a garage. The faint fumes of gasoline that might have lingered had been erased by new flooring and paint.

It was basically a single room with a counter divider and built-in shelves and cabinets, and a stove and half-sized refrigerator tucked into the corner by a glistening white sink.

The furniture was new, and it was expertly coordinated in gentle tones of honey and ivory, creating a calming, restful atmosphere.

"I think it might work for what you need," Jeannie said. "The furnace and water heater are behind this divider, and the kitchen and bathroom are pretty small but functional. Upstairs is the loft, where you can sleep if you want. This is a futon though, so you could sleep down here, too."

"It's awfully small," Hayden said.

Livvy laughed. "I used to have an apartment in the city that was about two-thirds the size of this, and it didn't have a loft either. I suspect you're just used to the dimensions of Sunshine, which seem to be endless."

"Well, speaking of small, I think you need to meet Leonard." Jeannie beamed proudly. "I believe that Hayden told you about him? He's my puppy."

Hayden snorted. "Puppy? Hardly!"

"You hush," Jeannie said, taking Livvy by the elbow and leading her out of the guesthouse. As they got close to the house, a series of deep woofs greeted them.

"Careful now," she warned as she opened the door. "Leonard loves people."

"For lunch," Hayden muttered, but Livvy knew he was kidding. At least she hoped he was kidding.

A gigantic dog launched himself at Jeannie, and she grabbed him by his collar. "Leonard, best behavior now! We have company."

The dog stopped and turned to look at Livvy. With a look of absolute glee on his furry face, he ran toward her, stood up, put his paws on her shoulders, and slurped his gigantic tongue across her cheeks.

She tried not to shudder. Dog slobber.

"Down, Leonard. Down!" Jeannie laughed as the dog obeyed. "See? He's a good boy. I can't take him with me to Africa, obviously, so he's part of the deal. You'd have to take care of him until I get back."

"I can do this," Livvy said, more to convince herself of it than to tell Jeannie. "I take him for a walk, I feed him. I can do this."

"He has to stay with you at night. He gets very nervous at night."

"He gets nervous at night," she repeated. "Excellent."

"That creature can't fit in there with her," Hayden objected.

Leonard looked up at Livvy adoringly, his head tilted to one side. She could have sworn the dog was smiling at her.

He really was quite cute, in a big dog sort of way. There was evidence of a terrier in his lineage, as evidenced by his short curly gray and brown hair and his long straight legs. A bit of Labrador retriever showed in his thick torso. The rest of him was bits and pieces of different breeds. All together, the dog was a mutt.

She didn't like dogs, not particularly. And certainly the thought of having one this size live with her inside the tiny little guesthouse was unappealing.

Then Leonard lifted one paw and placed it on her hand, very gently, very carefully, and her heart turned to mush.

"Okay," she said.

"Good!" Jeannie said, beaming at her. "Oh, look at you two. You're going to be best friends."

"Hayden and me?" Livvy asked, a bit taken aback.

"No. You and Leonard."

"He is a wonderful dog." Leonard gazed at her with liquid brown eyes, and she rubbed the soft spot behind his ears. "But my only worry is that I'll be out at Sunshine soon, that is, assuming that the moving is done and the renovations are complete."

Hayden cleared his throat. "Livvy, how long are you expecting all of this to take?"

She stood up, and Leonard came closer and leaned against her, nearly throwing her off-balance.

"I figure three weeks to get the place fixed up. I'll work on the outer buildings and the grounds and probably the swimming hole while you and your grandfather get resettled."

"Three weeks?" Hayden looked as if he had swallowed a toad. "Three weeks?"

"You can, of course, take as long as you need. My stuff is still on its way here, and it won't arrive for about a month, they told me at We Really Move You, since they have to pack everything up, too, so I don't have much to move in yet. You don't have to get everything moved out right away. I know there are many years of memories stored there, and I understand that."

It was amazing how well it was all working out. She congratulated herself on how quickly she had put it together in her head.

"How long are you giving yourself to fix up Sunshine, seriously?" he asked, his voice slow and even.

"Three weeks ought to be plenty."

He shook his head. "I think you need to back up on this. You haven't even seen the house except for the living room and the kitchen. For all you know, the rest of it could be a wreck."

"But it isn't, is it?" she asked stubbornly. She did not want to let go of this dream.

"I'm just saying—" He clapped his hand on his forehead and walked off.

"Honey," Jeannie said, her voice low enough that only Livvy could hear it, "this is a lot of money to invest. You need to be careful."

Livvy let her fingers trail across Leonard's ears and was rewarded with him rubbing his snout against her new black jersey slacks. She was sure that she now sported a line of dog goo across the fabric but she didn't care.

"I can trust them, can't I?" she asked, holding on as tightly as she could to the new life that Sunshine offered.

"Of course you can. But Gramps is old, and Hayden is a math teacher. Neither one is a carpenter or an electrician or a roofer. All they can do is chase after problems. You probably want to start over, tear out the plumbing, look at the wiring, investigate the heating system."

"I can do that."

"You can?" Jeannie's surprise was clear.

"Sure." Livvy watched Hayden pacing by the clothesline pole, clearly conflicted about something, and felt her resolution ebbing as totally as if someone had pulled the plug on it. Maybe hours of watching renovation shows on television hadn't prepared her after all. Her precious book, *The Complete Guide to Home Construction and Repair*, would help, but she knew it wasn't as complete as it proclaimed itself to be.

He pulled his Cooter's Hardware cap off, ran his fingers through his hair, and jammed the hat back on. And then he stalked over to Livvy and Jeannie.

"I never represented Sunshine as anything but an old run-down resort that has seen its time come and go, did I?"

"No," Livvy said in a little voice.

"And I never said it was in good shape, did I?"

"Well," she said, "you're living there with your grandfather, so I assumed it was livable."

"How are you going to get back and forth between Sunshine and Obsidian?"

"Trevor said—"

"Trevor wants an iPod more than anything. Keep that in mind whenever he's offering you a deal. That truck is held together with duct tape, putty, bubble gum, and a hot glue gun. Not to mention a whole lot of prayer—on the driver's part."

"I left my car at a lot to be sold before I left, but I can buy another one."

Jeannie coughed beside her as Hayden tore off his cap, ruffled his hair, and pulled it on again, this time with more vigor.

"When are you planning to do that?"

"Soon, I guess." She knew how bad this sounded, how unprepared she came across, but it was the truth.

"I don't know if I'd wait. That truck isn't going to make the trip between Sunshine and Obsidian too many more times before it becomes a permanent resident of the junkyard. That's where Trevor got the parts for it, I'm sure, so it'll be a homecoming of sorts."

She knew it was true. The truck made some pretty dire clacks and bangs, and she didn't even want to find out what shape the tires were in. She didn't have to wait—Hayden told her.

"And those tires—they're no better than balloons at this stage. Unsafe." He rubbed his chin thoughtfully. "Gramps has an old pickup out at Sunshine. It's not pretty but it's got four-wheel drive and it's a sight safer than Trevor's bucket of bolts. Let me make sure it's got good plates and registration. I think he kept it up but I want to be sure. If it's still good, we'll throw it in as part of the deal. I know Gramps doesn't drive it anymore, and I sure don't need it."

Four-wheel drive. She hadn't given much thought to the fact that she would probably be driving in winter.

As if reading her mind, Hayden continued, "You usually don't need four-wheel drive, but when you do, you're mighty glad you have it."

Jeannie nodded in agreement. "It's going to be a good idea,

Livvy, especially if you plan to winter out there. That's a long, lonely road from Sunshine into Obsidian, and sometimes it drifts over pretty badly."

Livvy swallowed. Hard. This was more than she'd thought about.

She tried to dismiss it. Winter driving didn't faze her. She'd managed Boston traffic in snow, and she could certainly make her way just fine on these uncrowded streets during winter. It wouldn't be that bad, would it?

"You could drive Gramps's pickup for a while. Whether or not you want to keep what you have, well, that's up to you and how safe you feel," Hayden said.

Her car was cute, a bright yellow little import that zipped through the city and was easy on gasoline. She loved it—in Boston. And now it sat at Buster's AutoWorld on the edge of the city, unless it had been sold to someone else. She'd miss it, but it wasn't what she needed here.

The fact of the matter was that Hayden was right. She had to do something about transportation, and Trevor's truck wasn't the answer.

"Thanks for the offer. Honestly, I'm delighted to return Trevor's truck to him. At least he's somewhat closer to his iPod, even if I don't keep the truck any longer."

"Good. I'll check into it. Well, we'd better get on with our errands if we're going to get a fishing pole in your hands this afternoon," he said.

"You're going fishing? That's lovely," Jeannie said. "The sun's burning off most of the rain, and it'll be pleasant. Use sunscreen, dear," she added in an aside to Livvy. "You'll burn worse than one of Alvin's pizzas if you don't."

"Alvin's pizzas?" she asked blankly.

"Alvin Johannsen owns Pizza World. His pizzas are legendary—for being crispy," Hayden explained.

She nodded.

The day was heating up, now that the drizzle had stopped. Overhead a lone cloud, wispy and thin, was stalled over the Badlands. Nothing else interrupted the space between the sky and the earth, save for the tops of the elms that brushed the endless blue. The sun touched everything, chasing away the shadows and warming roofs and sidewalks.

Cooter's Hardware. Alvin's Pizza. Clara's Café. It was a different world, and she was loving every light-drenched moment of it.

&

Hayden caught the door of the real estate office just before it slammed shut. Tom Clark, the agent, had assured him that the sale of Sunshine would be accomplished quite easily, and he'd draw up the papers that afternoon.

His stomach felt as if he'd swallowed a nest of wasps, buzzing and stinging inside him. This was probably the most important decision he'd ever made, encouraging Gramps to sell Sunshine.

It was for the best. He knew that. Gramps wasn't able to maintain it, and Sunshine deserved a better fate than falling into ruin.

He glanced at Livvy. Sunlight filtered through the leaves of the trees outside the agency, casting dappled pieces of sunlight across her dark hair.

She was so tiny.

He stopped himself. She wasn't tiny at all. She was sized just right. The top of her head came to his nose, which would put her lips—

He ended the thought before it went any further. Obviously he'd been out in the country too long, if that's where his mind was going.

She was buying Sunshine and that was it.

And, he reminded himself, once the papers were signed, it was hers. Totally hers. The only thing he and Gramps would own would be some of the glasses etched with the Sunshine name. . .and their memories.

He'd be off to teach, Gramps would be settled in a retirement home, and their lives, now intersecting with Livvy's, would head off in three different directions.

His mood began to disintegrate.

"You look sad," she said, her hand on his forearm, and her forehead wrinkled with concern. "This is rough, isn't it?"

He nodded, not trusting himself to speak for a moment. And then he gathered his emotions together and summoned a smile. "There's one sure way to chase away the blues," he said.

"Whistle?" She grinned.

"Actually I was thinking we could go fishing, but we can whistle on the way."

She looped her arm through his and the two of them began to walk to his car, trying to whistle and not laugh, and failing.

They spent the time traveling to Sunshine in the car, sharing songs they especially liked and those they absolutely hated.

"Some country," Hayden offered, "especially the old songs from the early days."

"Yes, Patsy Cline, for sure."

"A lot of classical, especially Bach."

"Bach's music is big—it takes over the room."

"Exactly! And Debussy is sweet."

"Sweet?" She tilted her head, questioning.

" 'Clair de Lune.' I have to confess though, that's the only Debussy melody I know. I took piano lessons when I was in grade school, and Miss Henrietta, my teacher, gave me 'Clair de Lune' to learn. I thought I'd never heard such a beautiful song." He smiled at the memory of sitting at the piano in his house, leaning over the keys, trying to find exactly the right phrasing for the song.

" 'Clair de Lune.' I haven't thought of that for ages! It's so pretty!"

"I played it so often that if my parents heard it on a store's audio, or on the radio, they clapped their hands over their ears. I suspect I didn't play it all that well, to be honest. I wasn't exactly a piano prodigy. I lasted through third grade, and then baseball called my name."

"I can see you playing baseball," she said. "You're a Red Sox fan, I hope."

"Sorry." He chuckled. "Around here pretty much it's the Twins all the way. Almost everybody supports the Minnesota teams, since North Dakota doesn't have major league sports. So it's the Twins for baseball, the Vikings for football, and the Wild for hockey—or the University of North Dakota in Grand Forks, of course—although hockey's so big here that local hockey is more important for most."

"I like hockey, but of course in Boston it's the Bruins that everybody roots for."

"It probably won't matter. You'll be a huge fan soon of the ObsMarWin team."

"ObsMarWin?" she asked.

"Obsidian-Martinville-Winston Consolidated School District, home of the Landers, which is short for Badlanders. It used to be the Badlanders but some kids got the bright idea to call them the Baddies, which wouldn't do at all, of course, so they became the Landers."

"The Landers. I like that!"

"They rarely get to the final rounds of any sports, but they play with all their hearts, and you've got to give them credit for that. You'll see folks around here sporting the green and gold as soon as the first puck flies."

"Green and gold being the Landers's colors, right?"

"Right. The school is here in Obsidian. It's that big prairie-style building we drove past on our way out of town. Sort of a sentinel here in the Badlands. I'll point it out on the way back."

The turn to Sunshine was still noted by a sign that had faded almost to the point of not being legible. How long had it been there? He didn't know. Since he was a boy, it had pointed the way to Sunshine. It had weathered everything from deep snows and blizzards to hot summer winds and blistering heat.

The sign, shaped like a smiling sun with once-rosy cheeks, was tilted to one side. Someone had probably taken the turn too sharply and clipped it.

He pulled over to the side of the road and tugged the sign back into place, shoring it up with one of the large stone chunks around the sign, there for that very purpose.

Livvy called through the open truck door, "That's a really cool sign. I'm surprised it's still here."

"I think Gramps just never got around to replacing it," he said as he put one foot on the running board and heaved himself onto the seat. "It's a bit out of the way for him, and I suppose other things were more important."

"I think it's charming," she said. "I meant though that I'm

surprised someone hasn't taken it."

"Why would they?"

"It's old and it's retro. It would probably sell for a lot of money. Don't you ever watch those antique shows on television?"

He shook his head. "I've heard of them but never watched them. We don't have cable at Sunshine."

"Oh, they're my favorites." Her face took on a dreamy, faraway look. "Those, and the home remodeling ones, and the travel programs. One day I'm going to go to Alaska and touch a glacier with my bare hands, and then I'll go to China and see the Great Wall and try to take in how big it is, and Egypt to look at the pyramids where I'll imagine what it must have been like during the days of the pharaohs."

"You like to travel?" He put the truck into gear and edged back onto the road, now headed toward Sunshine.

"I think I would."

He shot her a startled glance. "You haven't traveled?"

"This is as exotic as it gets for me."

He hooted. "North Dakota? Exotic?"

"It is, for someone who's spent her entire life in Massachusetts."

"You never left Massachusetts? I don't believe it." He avoided a rabbit that darted in front of the truck.

"Oh, I visited other New England states, but I never got much farther west than a ways into New York. But I've always wanted to see more of the world. Have you traveled much?"

"Not a lot. Minnesota, of course. Everybody goes to the Cities at some point."

"The Cities?" she asked. "Which cities?"

"The Cities are what we call Minneapolis and St. Paul. They're the Twin Cities, you know, so most people here simply call them the Cities. It's even capitalized, so if you see a reference to 'the Cities' and the *C* is uppercased, that's what it means."

"I see," she said. "I think."

"And I have gone into Canada, but not recently. It seems like every free minute quickly becomes not-free."

He rubbed his hand over his forehead, trying to erase the frown lines that he knew had carved themselves there. The truth was that Gramps had needed him more and more, and as it became clearer that the old man was edging toward heaven, he'd in fact needed his grandfather more. Needed to be around him, needed to hear his voice, needed to see him as much as he could.

Every August, when he'd had to start spending his days inside the big tan brick building preparing for school and then teaching, he'd hated being away from Gramps. And as the year slipped onward, from summer's blazing glory to unpredictable autumn, when there might be a forty-degree variable from one day to the next, he began to dread winter's arrival.

One day last winter, driven from desperation and exhaustion, he'd sent out applications to schools along the far southeastern coast of Florida. He could see himself with Gramps on the beach, soaking up the sun and the warmth and escaping the cold and the snow and the relentless wind.

But nothing had come of it, and he'd let it slip past, and here he was, heading into another school year, and he dreaded the deep winter that was coming.

He couldn't get out to see Gramps at night then—he often had school responsibilities that kept him in Obsidian—and the weekends were iffy at best. Usually the highway to the turnoff was clear, but after that, it was anybody's guess how bad the drifting might be.

Worry about his grandfather was never far from his mind.

"You spend most of your time with him, don't you?" she asked gently, startling him as if she had been reading his thoughts. "You don't have to say it. It's clear without the words. He's why you stay here."

"No!" he objected, perhaps more strenuously than necessary, and he immediately modified the word. "Well, not entirely. My heart is in Obsidian. It's in Sunshine, and it's in Gramps."

He refused to consider the day when he would not have either of them.

Fortunately he wasn't able to continue that train of thought, for when he pulled into the yard at Sunshine, Gramps was waiting for him, a fishing pole in each hand.

"Grub!" Gramps called, as he hobbled toward the truck. "I'm ready. Even dug up a nightcrawler or two." He gestured toward a tomato soup can in the shade by the front porch.

"You got us worms?" Hayden asked, taking the poles from his grandfather. "How did you do that?"

"I took that shovel over there"—the old man gestured toward a small camp shovel with a pointed tip—"and dug."

"Well, that's the way it's usually done," Hayden said. He walked over to the can where an earthworm was making its escape out the top of it. He dropped it back into the can, where three other worms were, and returned to the truck.

"I told Livvy we'd take her fishing."

"So we shall. There's an extra pole in the blue shed, and Grub, you'd better give her one of the canvas hats so she doesn't get burned."

Within minutes, Livvy was outfitted with fishing gear and

one of Gramps's old hats that was so big it insisted on sliding down over her nose.

"You can swim, right?" Hayden asked.

"Swim?" She had a look of faint panic on her face. "We're going swimming, too? I don't have a suit."

Gramps cackled. "The goal is not to go swimming."

"Not to—? Oh!" She laughed. "I can swim. I'm no Olympic gold medalist but I can get from one side of the pool to the other."

"There aren't sides to this pool. You need a life jacket," Hayden said. "They're in the boat. Let's go on down there and get things set up. I'll get the can of gasoline, and Livvy, why don't you grab that soup can? Those are the worms."

"Worms," she said faintly.

He had to smile at her reaction. "Not a worm fan, I gather. I'll put them on the hook for you."

She nodded. "I appreciate that."

Soon they were all at the boat, each one clad in a life jacket, smudged from being stored away, and thoroughly doused with bug spray. A blue and white cooler filled with root beer was tucked away next to the tackle box.

Hayden coaxed the small motor into life, and they headed out into the middle of the small lake. Sun sparkled off the water like reflected diamonds, and a light breeze ruffled the surface.

Hayden cut the motor, and the only sounds were of the river and the wind and the birds.

"Could you hand me the can of worms?" he asked, reaching for his fishing pole.

"Livvy, they're by your foot," Gramps said.

Hayden turned just in time to see the side of her pant leg

catch on the can, and it fell onto its side, spilling out dirt and earthworms.

For a split second, Livvy paused, and then she leaned over and quickly scooped everything back into the can, soil and worms alike.

"I'm impressed," he said. "Some women wouldn't do that."

She shook her head vigorously. "That is so old-fashioned. Most women could pick up a worm. We might not want to, but we'll do it."

"I thought you said you wanted me to put the worm on the hook for you," he said.

"Picking up a worm is one thing. Impaling it is another." She took the rod that Gramps handed her. "That is something I can't do."

"You don't have to use a worm," he said. "You can use a lure instead."

"Worms are good," Gramps said. "Fish are smart. They know food when they see it, and they know that a plastic thing with a hook hanging out of it isn't usually something to eat."

"Now, now," Hayden chided him gently. "You're a worm guy. I'm a minnow guy. Others insist that this lure or that is the way to go."

Gramps shook his head and muttered as he reached down, picked up a worm, and threaded it onto a hook.

Hayden grinned at Livvy. "I'm guessing you'd rather have a lure dangling on the end of your hook than a worm."

"Right you are. Show me how to do this, please. Is this one going to work?" She held up a bright green lure she'd taken out of the tackle box.

"Whether or not it works is up to the fish," he said. "If

it bites, it works. Doesn't bite? Doesn't work. Actually, you probably want this chartreuse one."

He leaned over her, and the faint scent of soap, clean and fresh, drifted through the sharp smell of the lake and the boat, of algae and fish and tarps.

Get a grip, he told himself. *You're in the middle of the lake with your grandfather, and this is the woman who's buying the ancestral home. And you've just had a talk about worms. Hardly the stuff of romance.*

He took her fishing rod and tied the lure onto the line. "You do it like this. See? You want it to stay on so you need to make sure it's pretty well knotted."

"Or else the fish will bite it and run away with it," she said.

"I don't think it'll run. Maybe swim."

"Okay, swim. So I tie it on. . ." She bent over the lure and examined it. "I can do that."

"Then you cast it as far as you can away from the boat, like this." He flicked the fishing rod back and forward, and the line swung out in a graceful arc. No matter how many times he did it, he loved the vision of the transparent line bowing across the water before settling under the lake.

"And then you wait." Gramps spoke from the other end of the boat.

"Hold on to your pole," Hayden added, giving her back the rod.

"Yup," Gramps added. "If it goes over, so do you. That's the rule of Sunshine. Otherwise we'd lose poles right and left. Can't afford to keep this place open if we have to buy new poles all the time. You kids, like Ellie said the other day. . ."

His voice trailed off, and Livvy shot a quick look at

Hayden, her brow briefly knotted with concern before she spoke again.

"What are we going to catch here?" she asked, leaning over the edge of the boat and peering into the water.

"Crappies and sunnies, usually. Sometimes a pike wanders in."

"Crappies, by the way, are spelled with an *a* even though you'd think they should be spelled with an *o* by the way the word is pronounced. I always explain that to people who are new to fishing up here."

Gramps laughed as he moved his line back and forth in the water. "Some folks get a bit upset when they see it in print, because it sure looks like a not-nice word. But it's pronounced *croppies*."

"Why?" she asked, resuming her seat on the boat again.

"Why are the folks upset, or why is spelled that way?" Hayden asked as he watched the line play in the water.

"The spelling. I know there's a fish called carp. I thought a crappie was a misspelled carp when I saw it in a magazine on the airplane."

Hayden had to laugh. She was so genuine. A misspelled fish!

"I don't know why it's called that. Do you, Gramps?" he asked his grandfather.

The older man shook his head. "Nope. It is what it is."

The fishing lines draped into the water, the filament looking for all the world like strands of silk in the sunlight.

The three of them sat in the boat, none of them speaking. The soft sighing of the poplars along the edge of the lake and the buzz of mosquitoes were a gentle backdrop to the quiet lap of the waves against the side of the wooden boat. In the distance, a bird called to an unseen companion, and a squirrel chattered angrily in protest of the interruption.

He loved this time, drifting idly in the boat on the little lake, thinking about the Creator and wondering why He would populate such a paradise with something as nasty as mosquitoes.

He slapped one that had managed to penetrate the DEET barrier, but he wasn't fast enough. He knew that within a short time, he'd be sporting a lump.

Eventually he'd have to start the motor again if Livvy was going to catch her fish. He hadn't had the heart to tell her that a lure didn't really work unless the boat was in motion, or if she wanted to cast and recast the line. He just wasn't ready to interrupt the mood with the sound of a motor. She'd understand.

He leaned back against the torn vinyl of the seat. Many summers ago he and Gramps had taken some of the dining room chairs that Gran had determined were too shabby for the public, and they'd cut the legs off and installed them in the boat. As Gramps had said, they weren't pretty but they were comfortable, especially if they wadded up the rain tarps and used them as pillows, and rested their feet on the rubber waders.

This was a little piece of paradise, Sunshine was. He'd often thought that if anyone didn't believe in a Creator, he'd just bring them out here on a boat on a summer afternoon. Nothing could quite compare to it.

He looked over at Livvy. Gramp's old hat had slid down on one side, and she made no attempt to straighten it over her still wildly curly hair. Instead, she smiled at the sun-speckled water.

Her fingers loosened their grip on the pole, and he caught back a smile. He'd watch it to make sure it didn't slip free.

If he watched closely enough, he was sure that he could see the stresses of city life falling from her, shed into the calm of the lake and absorbed by the water.

The pole slid a bit but she tightened her hold on it. Her manicure, he noticed, was still flawless. Within a short time, he suspected that would be a thing of the past.

Was she going to be able to do it? He had absolutely no doubt in his mind that she didn't have any idea what she was tackling here, but for some odd reason he was comfortable with that.

He thought back to the moment at the café when she'd pulled the hood off and her hair was tousled. She had looked real then, he'd said—real, natural, not citified.

Last night he had prayed about selling Sunshine to her, prayed long and hard. More than anything, he needed to be sure that what was about to happen was the right thing to do. There were precious few times in life that he'd wished to have the gift of seeing the future—usually it had seemed like a dreadful burden that no one would wish for—and he still didn't, but just some way of knowing selling Sunshine to Livvy was the right thing would have been so comforting.

But there were no answers, and he had to rely upon the feeling he'd gotten, that sense of prayer offered and answered. It was enough.

Sunshine would be in Livvy's hands and, most importantly, God's hands.

He turned and motioned to Gramps to hand him a root beer. It was part of their fishing tradition, having a root beer out on the lake.

There was something about being on the lake that made his grandfather seem less confused. He occasionally got a bit befuddled, but overall, sitting in the boat was good for Gramps. His mind rarely wandered when they were out on the water. Perhaps it was the calm, repetitive slap of the waves against the boat, and the gentle rocking motion. It certainly soothed him.

Gramps opened the cooler, took out a bottle, and tossed it to him. He twisted off the cap and was about to ask Livvy if she wanted one, when a sound stopped him.

It was ever so slight.

Livvy's eyes were closed, and she was faintly snoring.

Gramps grinned and nodded. "She'll be good for Sunshine," the old man said in a low voice. "Anyone who can fall asleep with a fishing pole in her hands has the heart it'll take."

"She won't catch anything with a lure," Hayden said. "She'll have to learn all that."

His grandfather studied him, his eyes bright with insight. "I think she's already caught something, Grub."

Hayden frowned and checked her line. "Nope, nothing."

Gramps just chuckled.

four

Livvy wiped her forehead with her arm and tried the wrench again. Tug as she might, the joint on the plumbing would not release. The basement of the house at Sunshine was cool, but she was frustrated. She'd been working on this leaking pipe for an hour with no luck.

That day of fishing seemed like three months ago rather than three weeks. So much had happened since her time with Hayden and Gramps on the lake. Now Sunshine was hers.

The men were still living there while she dog-sat Leonard. It was a nice arrangement. She was even beginning to appreciate having a dog around, although she wasn't sure that Martha Washington shared her feelings when they came to Sunshine.

Leonard would leap out of the truck and bound across the yard to the porch, his ears flopping crazily, as the resident chicken flapped back to the safety of the coop and Martha Washington stood and puffed into her formidable angry-cat shape. Leonard, having once met the wrath of the cat's claws, would temporarily abandon the overture of friendship and retire to the dirt next to the porch.

Sometimes that seemed like the best thing, soaking up the sun, and Livvy had done her share of it, but now she was determined to get busy with fixing up Sunshine.

She climbed down from the stepladder and consulted *The*

Complete Guide to Home Construction and Repair once again. The photographs were clear and would have been extremely helpful if the plumbing in this house had looked anything like the plumbing in the book.

Plus the man with the wrench in the illustration, who smiled happily as the pipes cooperated and came apart with ease, had apparently never met the plumbing at this place.

"How's it going?" Hayden asked as he came down the stairs. "Gramps said there was a leak down here and you were fixing it. You sure you don't want to call in a plumber?"

She pressed her lips together to stop the retort that arose almost immediately. "I can do it."

She wasn't about to tell him that she had been stuck on "Step One: Freeing the Pipe" the entire time.

He nodded. "Do you need any help?"

"No, but thanks. I have an idea though that will revolutionize the construction industry."

"What's that?" he asked.

"Putting the pipes on the floor. Hanging them from the ceiling makes this a horrendously uncomfortable task." She glared at the offending plumbing.

"I don't know if that would actually be much help," he said, walking toward her with caution. Tools and plumbing parts were spread across the cement floor. "But it's an intriguing idea."

"I went to Cooter's this morning," she explained. "Got my own toolbox and the parts I needed."

"I see that."

"There was a leak down here so I thought I'd start with something simple and fix it."

His mouth twitched with amusement. "Something simple.

That's a good idea. Are you finding plumbing to be simple?"

"How hard can it be? I mean, honestly. One pipe is connected to another pipe, which is connected to another pipe, and all I have to do is make sure that the water stays in the pipes and not on the floor, which is why I'm down here."

"That's about the best description of plumbing I've ever heard."

"Apparently though, whoever put these pipes up here stuck them together with some kind of super-powered glue." She glared at the maze of pipes overhead.

He shrugged. "Possibly."

"Anyway, I found out it was this one"—she tapped one with the wrench—"and sure enough, there was water coming from it."

She smiled at the book, which had given good advice on identifying the leak. "I turned on the water, came down here, and watched to see where it was dripping. And voilà!"

He nodded. "That's good. You remembered to turn off the water first, I hope, before trying to take the fitting off."

She resisted the urge to roll her eyes. "Of course I remembered. There's a diagram in here, on page sixty-four, of how to do that."

He nodded again, this time a bit slower. "It sure sounds like that book has it all. Do you mind if I take a look at it?"

"Go right ahead." Livvy made a face as a drop splashed on her shoulder. "Take a look at page sixty-four and tell me that's not wonderful. Meanwhile, I'll keep working on this—"

It happened all at once.

Hayden said, "Uh, Livvy," just as the coupling on the pipe gave way at last.

Water poured onto the floor.

"Pail! A bucket! Get me something!" she yelled as she retrieved *The Complete Guide* from the encroaching deluge.

Hayden ducked behind the furnace and returned with a large plastic trash bin that had earlier held a collection of unused pieces of drywall, bits of wood left over from a recent window replacement, and tiles that Hayden had pulled out of the old bathroom. "Remind me to clean that up later. I had to empty it onto the floor," he said as he moved it into place. "I'll be right back."

He took the stairs two at a time as she stood, watching in dismay as the container filled with water from the pipe.

How could this have happened? She opened the book and looked again at page sixty-four. She had done everything right. She'd turned off the water to the bathroom, hadn't she?

She opened her book and again scanned the section on plumbing repairs. There was no mention of anything like this. Nothing.

Oh.

There was one tiny line, almost lost in the diagrams. *"Turn off the water to the house."*

Well, why on earth did it tell her how to disconnect the water to the bathroom if she was going to turn it off to the entire house?

She wanted to sink to the floor and cry, but all that would do would get her pants wet.

She'd taken on way more than she—and *The Complete Guide to Home Construction and Repair*—could handle. Renovating a house was way beyond her capabilities. She couldn't even manage a simple plumbing repair without bringing on a flood.

On television it was so simple. Leaky faucet? A few twists

of a wrench and it was fixed. But maybe North Dakota had exotic plumbing—judging from the tangle of metal and plastic tubing in the ceiling joists, it had been put together by monkeys using leftover bits and pieces of plumbing. The whole thing should probably be taken out and redone.

But not by her.

It seemed like forever, standing in the basement and waiting for Hayden to come back. Maybe he'd left. After all, they'd signed the papers, she'd written the check, the title had cleared, and he had every right in the world to walk out of the house, get in his truck, and drive back to Obsidian, whistling the entire way. He and his grandfather were still living in the house until the housing for Gramps was set up, but there was nothing to hold them to being responsible for the antique plumbing woes that she was facing. She'd magnanimously taken that part out of the contract before signing it, telling herself that she could handle it herself.

The thought took root. Hayden was already out of the yard and headed down the county road, his grandfather beside him, and they were both delighted that he didn't have to deal with Sunshine's pipes.

Meanwhile she stood in a basement that was soon going to be filled with water unless she figured out something very quickly.

She scurried to the bottom of the stairs and called up, "Hayden? Hayden? Are you still there?" When she got no answer, she tried again, "Gramps? Gramps, did Hayden leave?"

Only silence answered.

She took a few tentative steps up. "Hayden? Gramps?" she tried again.

The house was silent. Even Leonard, who had come out from the house in Obsidian to Sunshine with her, didn't bark in response. That was not a good sign. Leonard barked at everything from a cricket to an airplane.

She bolted the rest of the way up to the main floor and quickly looked around. No one was there.

She'd have to call a plumber.

Her cell phone was in her purse, which was on the table upstairs. She bolted up the stairs and dug through her bag until she found the list she'd meticulously prepared using the phone directory that Jeannie had lent her before she left on her mission trip.

With nervous fingers, she unfolded the sheet of paper and found the listing for plumbers. She tapped the numbers onto her cell phone's keypad and heard. . .nothing. Silence.

She pulled the phone from her ear and glared at it. No wonder she couldn't get through—there weren't any bars on the display. There was no signal.

Hayden had mentioned that, and she'd forgotten it. She hadn't tried her cell phone at Sunshine before, and she put it on her list of things to get to: work out the telephone situation.

There was a telephone in the living room. She shook her head. *Way to be calm, Livvy*, she scolded herself. She'd totally spaced that out.

That telephone worked, wired nicely into the wall, and she picked up the receiver. How weird it felt to use this phone. It must be decades old. The handset was heavy and black, with a ridge along the top.

She dialed the first plumber on her list, and got a recording with the hours—they were not open on Saturdays or Sundays.

And this was a Saturday.

She tried the second number, and this time got someone. "Sunshine? You want me to come to Sunshine to turn off the water? Do you know how far I'll have to drive? Lady, that's going to cost you about $300 just to do that. You want it fixed, too? You're looking at $500, easy."

Leonard barked, a long series of happy sounds, and she sighed in relief. That meant that Hayden must not have left.

Silly her. Of course he wouldn't have gone off without telling her. She was just letting her imagination run away with her. She'd better nip that in the bud if she was going to stay out here all year round.

She realized that it had ended. The water had stopped. Hayden must have gotten the water to the house turned off. She breathed a deep sigh of relief.

She went back into the basement.

The mop was conveniently by the broken pipe. She'd been using it to swab down spiderwebs before her plumbing adventure. She shook her head as she remembered that her worst fear had been a spider dropping on her head. It should have been water!

She ran the mop over the floor. Luckily it was concrete, so she didn't have to worry about drying out carpets or warping wooden flooring. Most of the water she chased into a drain that was near the washing machine, and within minutes she was finished in the basement.

The best place for the wet mop was in the sun, where it would dry quickly, and she hurried up the stairs, holding it at arm's length, although she realized how pointless that was. She was pretty well splattered with water from the pipe.

The barking was closer, and she heard Hayden talking to

Leonard. "Settle down now. Yes, that's your ball. No, I won't throw it. Okay, I'll throw it. Now go find that dumb chicken to chase. Or Martha Washington. That worthless cat is probably asleep in the henhouse again."

She smiled to herself as she listened to him. It was like a dialogue.

"Leonard, no, I don't have time."

Bark.

"I said no. Well, just this once."

Bark bark bark bark.

There was a *thump*, which Livvy knew must be the ball hitting one of the outbuildings.

Bark bark bark.

"I have to go in and—oh, all right. But I'm serious, this is the very last time."

Bark bark.

With her elbow, she opened the screen door and propped the wet mop against the porch railing. "Hayden! Thank you so much!"

He paused, mid-throw. "Oh Livvy. I got the water turned off. I was on my way in to tell you when—" He gestured at the dog, who danced around him in gleeful anticipation.

"I understand. But what did you do that I didn't do, and would you please throw that ball before Leonard has a canine coronary?"

"What? Oh sure." He threw the ball and the dog tore off after it. "Doesn't he ever wear out?"

"Not that I've been able to tell. So how did you stop the water?"

"I used the turn-off to the house. Let me show you what I mean."

The dog followed them, yellow tennis ball still in his mouth and now covered with wet sand and dirt, as Hayden led her to the shaded side of the house.

"This," he said, pointing at a cement square set in the ground near the side of the house, "is where the main valve is. You pull on this handle, lift the cover, and there's the valve."

She shook her head. "I thought it would be inside."

"It should be, but we just never got around to it."

"Why wasn't it there in the first place? Why put it outside at all?" This made no sense to her.

"It's not uncommon out here with old houses that grew— or un-grew, if I can make up a word—without much design. There used to be a room in that spot, kind of a root cellar/ pantry/storage space, all rolled into one. At least that's what Gramps said."

"Ah," she said. Now it made sense. Sort of.

"That's actually something you should take care of quickly. Gramps and I got used to knowing where this was in winter, and how to keep the pipes from freezing, but you probably don't want to get involved with it. Let's get a plumber out here and have it moved."

She laughed slightly hysterically. "Get a plumber out here. And how do I do that?" She thought of the phone call she'd made earlier, and how she'd reeled at the estimate just to come to Sunshine. Dollar signs paraded through her mind, all of them leaving her nearly depleted bank account and headed into a plumber's wallet.

"You call someone."

"I did," she said. "He said it would cost at least $500. That was just to come out and shut off the water and fix the pipe. I can't even imagine how much he'd charge to move that inside." She motioned toward the red-handled valve.

He shook his head. "You have to know who to ask. There's a fellow from church who's a plumber and he's always worked on the barter system with Gramps. He's been trying to get Gramps to take care of getting the access to the water moved into the house for a long time. I'll tell you what, let me give him a call and see what we can work out."

Her stomach sank. She'd wanted to do this herself, but she couldn't.

"What do you mean by barter?" she asked. "Oh, I know what that means, but what do I give him in exchange?"

Hayden smiled. He really did have the best smile, she thought. It quirked up on one side, and his entire face lit up. "His name is Brad Simons, and he loves fishing, but he's got two sons, and one's in a wheelchair, so he doesn't get to do it much."

"Oh, I'm sorry to hear that."

"Usually I do the plumbing—and I have to apologize for the mess that you saw down there. That was my doing, and in case you couldn't tell, I had no idea what I was up to. I would just replace stuff until whatever was leaking stopped. One time I used a whole roll of aluminum tape, which works better than duct tape, by the way, so you might notice we buy the economy pack, to hold the kitchen faucet in place until Brad could get out here."

She laughed. "So you understand my plumbing skills—or lack of them."

"I do. In the past, we've worked it out so that Brad takes care of our plumbing emergencies and we get his family out here, all of them, and put them in the boat and take them out onto the lake."

"Really?"

"Really. Of course we'd do it for nothing, but Brad's got his pride. We do the whole day up right. We have a picnic on the boat, too, and then in the evening, we have a bonfire and roast hot dogs and make s'mores. It's a nice break for them."

"Do you suppose he would do this for me, too?" She was almost afraid to hear the answer.

"Sure he would. Let me give him a call right now. Here."

The dog was waiting patiently, the ball in front of his paws. Hayden picked up the ball and handed it to Livvy. It was slimy from being carried in his mouth, and she tried to suppress the urge to shudder. This was one of the things about dogs she'd never been comfortable with—the way they slobbered all over their toys.

"Gross," she said, wiping one hand on her jeans and holding the wet tennis ball gingerly with two fingers of her other hand.

He grinned. "Keep him busy while I run inside and give Brad a call."

He vanished inside the house as Leonard stood up, wagging his tail madly, his eyes locked on the ball in Livvy's hand.

"Okay, we'll do this until he comes back, but you really should get some hobbies," she said to the dog, and she threw the ball for him.

He raced after the ball, and loped back, carrying it in his mouth and dropped it at her feet. She tossed it again, he ran after it, and brought it back to her. Automatically she repeated the scene, and as she did, in her mind she ran through what it would be like out here, without Hayden and Gramps, without Leonard.

That day in Boston when she had brazenly given her

notice to Mr. Evans, the thought of being alone, responsible for a home that belonged to her, with no one around her for miles, had seemed like a dream come true.

Maybe she had taken on more than she'd bargained for, if the situation in the basement was any indication. Her beloved book, *The Complete Guide to Home Construction and Repair*, had misled her into thinking something as basic as fixing a leaky pipe would be easy.

Leonard flopped beside her, exhausted at last. His tongue hung out the side of his mouth, and he looked blissfully spent.

"What a life you have," she said to him. "As long as someone throws the ball and puts down dog chow for you, all is good. Every day is filled with nothing more important than sleeping in the sun and barking at squirrels. You don't even need to worry about your shoes or your hair or what you're going to wear."

His tail thumped and he sighed and shut his eyes.

She heard the screen door slam and turned to see Hayden coming back out. He gave her a thumbs up.

"Brad will be here in about twenty minutes. He said he could fix the pipe this afternoon, and on Tuesday he'll come out and move the shut-off valve inside. And it will only cost you an afternoon on the lake and a weenie roast, due and payable next Saturday, while he and the missus go to a wedding. I said we'd watch the boys. By the way, it's the Fourth of July, so we'll do fireworks out here, too."

"Fireworks? That's good, but it just doesn't seem quite enough," she objected, feeling relieved and at the same time vaguely guilty. "Is that a fair trade?"

"It is for Brad. He's got a lot on his plate. Speaking of

plates, Gramps got some sandwiches ready for us."

They had just finished a meal of peanut butter and jelly sandwiches and root beer when a horn honked in the yard.

"Brad's here," Hayden said, draining the last of his drink.

She thought she'd never seen anyone as welcome as Brad with his plumbing tools. In his work shirt and heavy boots, he looked like an angel.

He followed her into the basement and then indicated he wanted her to stay. "Stick around," he said to Livvy. "I'll show you what you need to do."

As he fixed the pipe, he told her what he was doing every step of the way in a running commentary. "Don't blame yourself," he said as he tightened it into place. "It's just a lot easier if someone shows you how to do it. It's not brain surgery but it does have its quirks. There. See how it's done?"

She nodded, but made a mental note to proceed more carefully in the future when it came to plumbing.

"Now," he said, putting the wrench back into his toolbox, "I'll turn the water back on. Come with me, and I'll show you that, too."

Outside, he gave the red valve a twist, saying, "And the next time anyone touches this dumb thing will be the last time. You'll never have to worry about finding it out here again."

"How can I ever thank you?"

"It's all in a day's work. I'll go check on the pipe and say howdy-do to Charlie and then I'd better get back to town. See you tomorrow."

"Tomorrow? I thought you were coming on Tuesday."

"Won't you be in church? It's Sunday, you know."

"Oh. Of course."

As he went into the kitchen to visit with Gramps and Hayden, she thought about it.

Church.

She wasn't a churchgoer, not recently. How long had it been since she'd been to a service? She did some quick math and was aghast to realize it had been about ten years. Almost a decade.

It wasn't as if she didn't believe in God. Of course she did. Everyone did. How many times had she looked at a sunset, or a newborn baby, or a kitten, and acknowledged the good work of the Lord's hands?

But it was also true that the only times she prayed anymore were when she was petitioning God to let her car start or when her wallet wasn't where it should be. Certainly there was more to being a Christian than that.

She looked at the majestic panorama of the Badlands surrounding her. This had to be more than a geological accident. Someone had to have created this interplay of shape and light and color.

God? Could it be?

A hunger gnawed at her heart. She needed to know more.

The voices of the three men in the kitchen floated out to her. They all went to church. Maybe she should give it a try. What could it hurt? Nothing. And what could it help? Everything.

Her life was fine the way it was, but maybe it could be better. She'd ask Hayden about it.

Leonard, who had gotten up and come to lie across her feet, moved, nudging the ball that never left his side.

"What do you think, dog?" she asked, leaning over to let her fingers drift over his silky ears. "Dogs don't go to church."

"He would if he could," Hayden said behind her, and she jumped. "Sorry, didn't mean to startle you. Brad's leaving now, and I gather the plumbing emergency is taken care of. You up to digging through some boxes in the café? I suspect most of it can go to the dump, but let's make sure."

They headed toward the café, the dog padding behind them.

"You all go to the same church?" she asked.

"Sure do. We're all members of Trinity. My great-grandfather was one of the founders of it. Would you like to come to a service?"

"You know, I think I would."

"What church did you go to in Boston?"

Something rustled in the underbrush, and Leonard took off, barking at it.

"I didn't go to church there," she confessed. "I don't know why. Partially I was just lazy, but it's also a bit overwhelming trying to decide which one to go to."

"Obsidian doesn't offer many choices," he said. "There's Trinity. Or there's Trinity. Yup, that's it."

She laughed. "Then Trinity it is."

He tilted his head and smiled, his pale blue eyes glinting in the sun. "Would you like to go to church with us? We'd be delighted to have you there."

"I think I would," she said, and as soon as the words were out, she felt a peace. "Yes, I would."

"Great! I'll talk to Gramps. He'll think it's a wonderful idea."

"Speaking of wonderful ideas," she said as they reached the door of the café, "let's start digging."

They worked together, going through the boxes that had been

stored in the dusty café. As Hayden had predicted, most of the boxes were filled with things not worth keeping. Three of the cardboard cartons contained draperies that had been the home of small creatures, probably mice. Two more boxes held tablecloths, now stained with age, and one box was filled with packets of paper napkins. These were easily set aside to be discarded.

Hayden moved another stack of cartons to the middle of the room. "We'll tackle these next week. I don't know about you, but I'm done."

"Me, too." She wanted nothing more than to clean herself up and sprawl on the couch of the little guesthouse in Obsidian and let the air-conditioning cool her off.

"If you'd like," he said to her, "I'll pick you up tomorrow for church."

"I'd like that." Just knowing that she wouldn't have to walk in alone made it easier to decide to go.

"Great. Church starts at nine thirty, so I'll see you around nine fifteen."

As she drove back to Obsidian in Gramps's SUV, which was a sight better than Trevor's truck, she looked at her surroundings, once again astonished at the panorama laid out around her. With something as spectacular as the Badlands as a backdrop to her new life, it was only fitting that she should offer praise to their Maker.

Church. She was going to church.

&

Hayden was used to the church, but now he was seeing it as he imagined Livvy would. How different it must be from the grand cathedrals and massive churches she probably saw on every street in Boston.

Trinity was a small white-framed structure, basically

unchanged in its 125 years of existence. The interior showed the importance those first church members had assigned their place of worship. A large mural of the Nativity adorned the wall behind the altar, and its hues were still as bright as they must have been when they were first painted. Stained-glass windows, handmade by an early settler to the town, shed multicolored beams on the tiny congregation.

Hayden could feel Livvy's uneasiness as they slid into the pews. He was so accustomed to coming to church every Sunday that it had never occurred to him how awkward it might be for someone not used to attending services to visit for the first time.

He smiled encouragingly and whispered, "I'm glad you're here."

"Thanks," she answered in a low voice. "I'm glad I'm here, too."

The hymns and Scripture readings were marked on the board at the front of the church, but there was also a bulletin. He noticed that she studied it closely, especially the announcements of the upcoming Men's League barbecue, and the Women's League garage sale.

He hadn't been involved much recently in the Men's League, and he reminded himself to make it to the next meeting. Maybe Gramps would like to be a part of it, especially since he would be moving into town.

The minister, Reverend Carlisle, stood in front of the congregation and motioned for them to rise for the first hymn. It was one of Hayden's favorites, "Faith of Our Fathers."

He loved the old hymns. Singing the same melodies and the same words as his forebears had done gave him a sense of connection with the past that he treasured. He heard Gramps's wavering tenor next to him, and he put his hand on the old man's shoulder, and was rewarded with a smile.

He could sing the hymn from memory, but he held the hymnal with his free hand so that Livvy could see it, too. She followed along well, her clear soprano melding with the others in the congregation, and he could feel her relax.

At the end of the song, they sat and the minister shared the day's gospel lesson with them. It was the very beginning of Luke. "*Forasmuch as many have taken in hand to set forth in order a declaration of those things which are most surely believed among us, even as they delivered them unto us, which from the beginning were eyewitnesses, and ministers of the word; it seemed good to me also, having had perfect understanding of all things from the very first, to write unto thee in order, most excellent Theophilus, that thou mightest know the certainty of those things, wherein thou hast been instructed.*"

It was, the minister pointed out, a passage about history and faith. It was the faith of their fathers, just as the hymn had extolled, that brought them to this point of being gathered together this Sunday. Luke had his own forefathers of the church to build upon, and he had drawn upon that in his own faith journey—and what a journey it was.

Who, Reverend Carlisle asked, was Theophilus? Was he simply someone to whom Luke was writing?

The name, he explained, meant either *lover of God* or *loved by God*. Was there a difference?

The part of his name, *Theo-*, meant God. In addressing the letter to someone named Theophilus, Luke was passing his own religious heritage.

The people he was about to share with Theophilus were those who been there from the beginning, who were, as Luke said, eyewitnesses.

Reverend Carlisle leaned forward. "And dwell, if you would, for a few minutes on the last of this passage: 'That thou mightest know the certainty of those things.' Think of it. The certainty. Luke was solidly convinced of the truth of faith, and that is what we all need, knowing with certainty that God is true, that faith is true, that His love for us is true."

Hayden saw Livvy lean forward as if trying to absorb the message. Sunlight, dyed by the stained-glass windows, tinted her hair and face with blues and greens and purples.

"And when we know that this is true, that is faith. Loving God and being loved by God is an inheritance that is beyond anything we might get here on earth," the minister continued. He beamed at those gathered in front of him. "Sure beats Aunt Ethel's silverware or Uncle Ole's letter from the president, doesn't it? Not to say that those aren't important, but. . ."

He let the thought trail off as the congregation took in the meaning.

Hayden let the idea of faith and love as an inheritance settle into his mind, and through the rest of the service, he considered it. He'd always been proud of his great-grandfather for being one of the founders of Trinity, but now there was more to it. Now he was also grateful.

Too soon the congregation was standing again, and the church service was over. He turned to Livvy as the recessional began and the congregation began to chat with each other in low voices as they filed out of the small church.

"So what did you think?" he asked. He was surprised at how important her answer was to him.

"It was wonderful," she said, her face glowing. "I felt like a dry sponge in water, soaking it up."

"It was good, wasn't it?"

Gramps leaned around him and added, "I'd never thought about that part of Luke before. Grub, if you don't mind, I think I'd like to go home and study this a bit more."

Hayden looked at his grandfather in surprise. Usually they went to Clara's after church for an omelet and coffee. Gramps looked tired and drawn, as if the service had worn him out. Hayden's heart dropped. This was not good.

Livvy took the gnarled fingers of the old man in her own as they walked out of the church. "I think we all could use some time for reflection. I can walk back to my place."

Hayden wanted to object, but he could see a slight tremble in the old man's shoulders. It was a time of change, and it had clearly taken its toll on him.

"If you don't mind," he said.

"Not at all. I need to get home to make sure that Leonard hasn't gone off in search of Jeannie. After all, she's in Africa, and that's quite a walk, even for him."

He smiled despite his worry. Her words lightened his heart a bit, and he was appreciative to her for that.

"I'll see you tomorrow then."

He watched her walk away, and he turned his attention to Gramps, who nodded slowly. "She's a good one, Grub. Don't let her get away."

"She's just going to Jeannie's guesthouse, Gramps. She's not going far."

The twinkle came back to his grandfather's eyes as he said, "That's not what I mean, and you know it. She's the one for you."

"I don't—I barely know—we just met," Hayden stammered.

"Remember what Reverend Carlisle said. Certainty. It

extends outside the church walls, Grub. Have a little faith. No, have a lot of faith. Have a lot of faith."

Hayden hugged the old man's shoulders lightly. "I do, Gramps. I do."

five

Livvy walked to her little house, mulling over the worrisome tremors she'd felt in Gramps's hands. He'd looked especially frail when Hayden had picked her up, but she had chalked that up to the suit he wore. Maybe it had fit him once, when he was more muscular, but now it hung on him. Still it was sweet, she thought, the way his shirt was pressed and his tie neatly knotted. Church obviously meant a lot to him.

But when they'd left the service, his face had been pale, and his movements feeble. She had to trust Hayden's judgment. He'd take him to the small hospital if he felt Gramps's condition warranted it.

She wanted to pray for him. More than anything, she wanted him to be healthy and whole and not sick at all.

The thing was, she couldn't pray like the ministers did. She had never been able to figure out what the difference was between *thee* and *thou*. But Reverend Carlisle hadn't used those words. He had simply talked to God.

She could do that. Her attempts were halting. *Make him better, God. You know what he needs. Please get it to him. Make whatever is wrong, right.*

It wasn't pretty, it wasn't magnificent, it wasn't long. But it stated what she wanted.

Leonard barked happily when he saw her coming down the block, and she had to restrain him from knocking her over out of sheer glee when she opened the fence and came into the yard.

"I was gone an hour, you goofball," she said as she unhooked the tether from his collar so he could run freely in the yard. "A whole hour. During which you managed to knock over your water dish, spill your doggy doodles on the grass, lay across your mommy's prize rosebush, and dig a hole right next to the birdbath. You're a busy boy."

She repaired the damage as well as she could, and let him come in with her to the guesthouse. He flopped beside her as she stretched out on the futon. It wasn't that she was tired, she just needed some time to rest and reflect.

"This isn't made for both of us," she said to Leonard. "One of us is going to have to concede defeat and get up."

The dog simply sighed and settled even more deeply into the cushions.

"Well, there is something to be said for peaceful coexistence." She pushed him as far to the edge as possible, and laid on her back, staring at the ceiling fan.

She'd actually gone to church. It wasn't as if she ever had anything against going to church. It was just that her family hadn't made it a priority. They usually went when she was a child, but there wasn't much of a reason behind it. They went because they were expected to.

She rolled off the futon and retrieved her laptop. As she opened it, Leonard flung himself across the rest of the cushions. She wasn't getting back on without some pushing of doggy flesh.

Jeannie had thoughtfully continued the wireless account, and Livvy was soon able to connect with her mother.

"So," Mrs. Moore began, "how's life in North Dakota?"

Livvy laughed and told her the story of the plumbing,

lightening it up so it sounded comedic—although, in retrospect, it was really kind of funny. Then she said, "Mom, guess what. I went to church today."

"Good! Did you like it?"

"I did. It made me feel peaceful, and yet there was a lot to think about, too. I'm going to go back."

"That's wonderful, honey! Did I tell you that your dad and I found a church here, too? We went initially just to see what a Swedish church service was like."

"Was it different?"

Mrs. Moore laughed. "Well, it's in Swedish. It's interesting, attending services when you aren't a native speaker. Your father and I have to listen to each single word."

"I thought you two were completely fluent."

"Not totally. We're competent but there are some gaps, especially in the Old Testament language. So we take both Bibles, Swedish and English. You don't suppose that's cheating, do you?"

Livvy chuckled. "Somehow bringing two Bibles to church couldn't be construed as cheating, I'd say."

"That's true! I hadn't thought of that. Actually," her mother said with some surprise in her voice, "I'm learning more about God by hearing the words in a language not my own. I hate to say this, since I'm a teacher, but it's amazing what you can learn if you listen to every single word."

So her parents had come back to the church. Her mother continued to talk of her social activities, and ones at the church were mixed with those from the school, or those with her friends.

Livvy thought of the Women's League garage sale she'd seen in the bulletin. Certainly in those boxes stored across the property at Sunshine were some things that she could donate—with Hayden and Gramps's permission—and that might be fun, getting involved with the women of Trinity. It would be a great way to meet people and make some friends.

After all, Sunshine was fifteen miles out of Obsidian. It wasn't like she would have a next-door neighbor to drop in and have a cup of coffee with. Even Hayden and Gramps would be gone.

Leonard sighed in his sleep, and when she ended the conversation with her mother, she returned to the futon.

She threw her arm across Leonard. He moved and pressed against her even more tightly.

There was something very calming about lying on the futon, squished between an oversized dog and the back cushions. She should get up, make some lunch, run the towels through the washing machine, and pay some bills, but all that could wait.

This was Sunday, and her soul was at rest, and soon, so was she.

&.

Hayden folded the dish towel and hung it on the rack by the sink. Lunch had been a thrown-together meal, lunch meat and cheese on bread, with pudding for desert. Afterward, Gramps had retired to his recliner, where he promptly fell asleep.

His grandfather was snoring softly and evenly, but Hayden was still concerned. Reluctant to leave Gramps alone, he tiptoed back into the living room and sat on the old green sofa. In the light that filtered through the windows, he saw how threadbare it was.

It had been there for as long as he could remember. What

was the lifespan of a sofa anyway? This one had been a bed when he'd been a small boy.

It was odd, he thought, how he'd never noticed how loudly and how relentlessly the old anniversary clock on the mantel ticked. The sound seemed to fill the living room.

He wiped away a thin layer of dust on the table beside him. No matter how hard he tried, there was no way to keep the place clean, not with the wind that seemed to find every crack and gap in the house. It was amazing that the Badlands hadn't been reduced to nubs with the seemingly constant wind.

He crossed his legs and crossed his arms and uncrossed his legs and uncrossed his arms. How did people do this sitting-quietly thing? In church it was easy enough, but here, with nothing to look at but the Norman Rockwell painting by the fireplace and the little stuffed Teddy Roosevelt bear propped against the lamp on the end table, it was impossible.

He was forced to think. First about Gramps—how could he ever go on without him at his side? His grandfather had been woven into his life from his birth. For as long as he could remember, Gramps had been there for him. It had been Gramps who'd taught him about baiting a hook—that it wasn't a simple matter of sticking a worm on the barb and dropping the line into the water.

He smiled at the memory of floating on the little lake in the boat—the same boat that he and Gramps had taken Livvy out in, except it had been newer and its paint fresher. That afternoon had been filled with root beer and peanuts. Gramps insisted the turtles liked peanuts, although Hayden never saw a turtle eat a peanut. Instead, he and Gramps swigged root beer and tossed the peanuts in the air, trying to catch them in their mouths and usually failing.

Gramps had shown him the fine art of choosing a lure based upon what he wanted to catch. "Minnows, worms, or leeches for crappies, sunnies, or perch. Watch the water temperature. Warm water, you can use a lure."

He'd opened the tackle box and showed Hayden the contents. The lures were as fascinating as a treasure chest. Silvery jointed metal fish were laid neatly next to feathery hand-tied creations. Delicate flies were adjacent to brightly tasseled jigs. Lifelike frogs and ribbony strings—he had never seen anything as intriguing as this tackle box.

"This one's neat," Hayden had said, lifting up a bright orange jig, the tassels dancing in the sunlight. "I like it."

"It's pretty but it's not worth much here. You want the lure to be as close to the color of the natural bait as possible. Is there anything orange here that a fish might eat?"

Hayden recalled how sad he'd felt that the brilliant lure was basically worthless, and apparently his grandfather had noticed, because he'd squeezed the boy's shoulder and said, "You'll have a lot of shiny orange lures in your life, Grub. Just remember that a shiny orange lure may not be what you want or what you need."

It hadn't made sense then, but over the years, he'd come across many shiny orange lures, and Gramps's wisdom had come through.

He looked over at him, asleep in the chair.

Livvy wasn't a bright orange shiny lure.

His mind danced around the vision of Livvy in church, and Gramps's words came back to him. *The one.* Was Gramps right again? Was Livvy the one for him, the one with whom he could spend a lifetime?

How would he know?

He'd always heard Gramps tell how when he first met Gran, she thought he was boring and dull, definitely not a bright orange jig. If anyone had told him they'd end up married and loving each other with each breath, right up until she drew her last, he'd have said they were nuts.

But so it had happened, and a great love had been born and endured.

Was it Hayden's time for an equally great love?

He had no idea. It was too early to know any of this.

The clock ticked, and his grandfather snored, and he realized that they were creating a rhythm together. His toes tapped silently, the left foot marking time with the clock and the right foot keeping pace with Gramps.

Was it possible? Was the clock ticking louder?

He couldn't stand it. He stood and crept back into the kitchen where he opened the refrigerator and took out a bottle of root beer, wincing as it hissed when he opened it.

The *Bismarck Tribune* was on the front seat of the car. He could read that.

The loose board on the kitchen floor creaked when he stepped on it, and he paused, but Gramps snored on. He went outside, catching the screen door before it could slam, and reached into the truck through the open window to retrieve the newspaper.

He repeated his silent path back to the living room, and sat down once again on the green sofa. Martha Washington, who had somehow managed to sneak inside, leaped up next to him and began to purr so loudly Hayden thought for sure that Gramps would awaken, but he slept on.

The paper had never sounded as crinkly. He spread the

open paper on the coffee table and tried to turn the page, slowly, carefully, and he thought he had almost made it when his grandfather sat up and said, "Why are you being so sneaky quiet?"

"As soon as I scrape myself off the ceiling, I'll answer you. You nearly scared the wits out of me."

"Sorry," his grandfather said. "But why are you tiptoeing around like a thief?"

"I didn't want to wake you up. Gramps, are you feeling all right?"

Martha Washington sprang from the sofa to Gramps's lap, and the old man smoothed the cat's fur. "I'm fine. I was feeling a bit rocky this morning, but I think it was just because I didn't sleep that well last night."

Hayden crossed the room quickly and leaned over his grandfather, solicitously feeling his forehead for a fever. "You didn't sleep well?" he fretted. "You usually sleep like an absolute rock."

"An absolute rock, huh?" Gramps asked, his lips twitching in amusement. "Compared to a non-absolute rock? An inabsolute rock? What?"

Hayden knew the teasing was an attempt to divert him from pursuing the subject further. His grandfather did look better after his nap. He also knew better than to pursue the issue at the moment. When Gramps didn't want to talk about something, he shut down the topic.

Instead, Hayden would have to watch Gramps closely to see if he could pick up any clues about what had happened. Maybe it was nothing, but he didn't want to take the chance of dismissing something major.

He matched his grandfather's light tone. "Plymouth Rock.

A moon rock. Rock of Ages. I don't know. But I should tell you I debated throwing that clock into the lake. That thing ticks so loudly it almost blew out my eardrums."

Gramps laughed. The sound was like music to Hayden's ears. It meant he was truly feeling stronger and better. "Once you're aware of it, it does seem to get extremely loud. Your grandmother put it out on the porch one time when she was trying to read. She could still hear it, so she put it out in the middle of the road by the mailbox. She said it made such a racket, she couldn't take it anymore. Lucky the thing didn't get run over."

Hayden wasn't convinced that *lucky* was the appropriate word for such an obnoxious creation, but he didn't say anything about it.

"Church was good today, wasn't it?" Gramps asked. "That Reverend Carlisle sure can dig out a deep meaning from the gospel. I dare say he's so good he could have one of those big congregations in Chicago or Minneapolis."

"We are truly blessed to have him here in Obsidian."

"Livvy seemed to enjoy the service, wouldn't you say?" Gramps looked directly at him. "She seemed to drink it up like a thirsty woman at an oasis."

Hayden folded the newspaper and leaned back. "She did. You know, Gramps, we were born into the church and we stayed. You and Gran made sure of that, and that's part of the heritage that Reverend Carlisle was talking about."

"I'm as old as Luke?" His grandfather's eyes twinkled.

"Pretty much," Hayden answered, grinning. "But I think that part of what the lesson was about is that our religious legacy goes back to the very beginning of Christianity—and before—so that even if we have a few years when we stray, we've got the path already prepared for us to step right back onto."

"That's an interesting extension of what we learned today." Gramps stroked Martha Washington's fur. "We tried to make sure you knew where the path was, Grub, so that if you did step off, you could be sure that it was there, ready and waiting for you. But we were fortunate that you stayed on it, and you've lived a life that was honorable to our Lord."

"I've tried." As Hayden said the words, he knew they were true. "I don't think that Livvy has done anything wrong, even if she hasn't been going to church."

His grandfather raised his eyebrows in question, and Hayden hastily amended his statement. "I mean that she hasn't murdered anyone, at least as near as I know."

Gramps laughed. "I think we can safely presume that she hasn't. She doesn't seem the type to be a felon. But going to church is an important part of being a Christian. And I think she realized that."

"She seemed to get a lot out of the message this morning. I'm glad she went with us."

"I suspect she needed it. We'll make sure to invite her to come with us next week, too." His grandfather studied him. "You know I'm not one to meddle in your life, Grub, but I do need to say something."

Hayden took a deep breath. Whenever Gramps started a discussion like that, the conversation was going to be intense—and honest.

"Go ahead," he said. "Meddle away."

His grandfather bent toward him, his face etched with concern. "I want to talk about Livvy."

Hayden's stomach plummeted. Did Gramps have second

thoughts about turning Sunshine over to her? It was too late. The papers were signed, and she was already invested in the property, both financially and emotionally.

"What about her?" he asked cautiously.

"I may be old, but I can still see what's right in front of my face. There's something between the two of you."

Hayden rubbed his forehead. "Something between us? How can you say that? I've only known her a few weeks!"

"How long do you think it would take?" Gramps looked at him quizzically.

Hayden cleared his throat, which had inexplicably developed some kind of frog. "Well," he said at last, "a year or two."

"And when do you think it starts?"

Gramps was not going to let him off easily. Hayden parried with another question. "Do you mean when does love start?"

"Sure. When do you think people fall in love? What is the first moment? Does it hit you like a two-by-four upside the head? Or is it a gentle thing that comes over you, so slowly that you don't even know it's happening until one day you find yourself in front of a preacher saying, 'I do'?"

Gramps's tone was teasing, but underneath it was a serious note, and Hayden waited a moment before answering. "I'm not sure, Gramps. I've never been in love."

His grandfather nodded sagely. "It happens both ways. Love takes awhile to develop, and I'm not saying this is love that I see. Not yet. But given enough time, and enough care, I believe that this attraction between you two has the power to grow. Not all relationships do, but this one, I believe, does."

"Do you believe in love at first sight?" Hayden asked.

"I do, but with a rider. There is love at first sight, but love has to prove itself—no, wait. That's not right. Love never has to prove anything. Love is perfect and ideal. Let me try again. There is such a thing as an immediate attraction."

Gramps's eyes took on a faraway, dreamy look. "When I first saw Ellie I was a gas jockey in Bismarck. I was in that never-never land after school, not knowing what I wanted to do, and thinking that maybe I'd end up enlisting in the army. All my friends were doing it. And then one day, she drove into the station in a brand new 1957 Chevy. Grub, that thing was a magnificent piece of automotive history. Turquoise and white, and absolutely spotless."

Hayden settled back against the cushions of the couch. He'd heard the story before, but it was a great one.

"I looked at it, and I was going to say all the usual gas station things about the car. Ramjet fuel injection, triple turbines, V-8, rear fins, hood rockets—and then I looked at her, and all of that just flew out of my head. She may have been sitting in the most stunning car to grace America's roads, but all I could think was that she was the most beautiful woman I had ever seen and, bam, I was in love."

"So it was love at first sight."

"It was. But it wasn't the love that developed over the years. We had to learn to love each other, and, perhaps just as importantly, learn to be loved in an equal relationship. In order for a marriage to work, you need to have the same set of values. You can't be unequally partnered. If you believe in God, and I know you do, then she has to believe in Him, too. That's vital. Without that, there really won't be love. Marriage has to have some basis or else it won't last. Grub, you know where the silver is, don't you?"

Hayden laughed. "Well that was an abrupt switch. From love to silver."

"Don't be fresh. Go get it. But first go get me a spoon from the kitchen."

From the strength of his grandfather's voice, he knew that there would be some meaning in this lesson, so he did as Gramps requested. From the kitchen he got a spoon from the drawer, and then he entered the dining area.

He crossed the room to the old Hoosier cabinet that still stood in the corner, just as it had for as long as he had been alive, and from one of the drawers, he withdrew a polished walnut box and carried it back to his grandfather.

Gramps carefully balanced it on his thin knees and opened it. He removed the cloth that covered the silverware, and took one of the spoons from its slot.

He held it up to the light. "We got this for a wedding present from your great-great-grandmother. See the glow of it? See how you can look at it and immediately know that it's good silver? Look at the patina. That satiny finish comes from years and years of use, scooping up food and who knows what else, as well as being scrubbed clean and stored away and ignored for months on end."

His grandfather tapped it against his hand. "That shine comes from years of Greenwood family dinners. And it's heavy. You can feel it in your hand when you're eating your ice cream."

He put it back into the slot in the wooden box and closed the cover reverently. He picked up the spoon from the kitchen and raised it. "Now this is the cheap stuff, the stuff we don't care if the dishwasher mangles it or if it gets left in the boat. It can easily be replaced with a quick trip into

Bismarck to that big discount center."

The spoon caught the afternoon sun and sent rainbows against the wall. "Pretty, isn't it? Glittery and bright," Gramps continued, "but cheap. Even I could bend it, warp it out of shape. Scratches on the surface just make it look worse, and if its life as a spoon is too bad, we'll throw it away and get another one. And why is that?"

"Because we don't care about it, not really," Hayden answered. "It's from that set we got at ThriftyBuy for what, fourteen dollars?"

Gramps shook his head. "Sort of. Because the wedding silver is made out of quality metal and the everyday spoon is made of, well, I don't know what it's made of, but that's my point. Do you see what I'm saying? Love is like the wedding silver. The good and the bad will both add to the gleam, compared to the sharp imitation-silver spoon that can't bear any scratches. It's disposable, so we can get rid of it when we're not pleased with it."

He handed the day-to-day spoon back to Hayden. "You know, when the silverware was new, it was shiny. Not quite this wildly shiny, but shiny. I liked it shiny, but I like this subdued gloss, too. That's love. From new-spoon shiny to old-spoon gleam, it's all good."

Hayden impulsively leaned over and dropped a kiss onto the top of the old man's head. He wasn't quite ready to think of marrying Livvy, but this was excellent advice. "I'll give it some thought and a lot of prayer, Gramps, I promise. You may be right about Livvy—or you might be wrong. Either way, I need to make sure of one thing."

"What's that?" Gramps asked.

"That she's the right spoon."

six

The Fourth of July was a jewel of a day. The faintest breeze blew away the dusty heat, until it was nearly perfect. Brad had come out with his two children, Bo and Al, and the three of them had crowded into the boat with Hayden and Gramps.

Brad's wife was, according to him, "dollying up" in preparation for a wedding in Bismarck that evening, and Brad was going to leave the boys for fireworks while he went to the wedding with his wife. He'd pick the children up around midnight.

The boys had reveled in their afternoon on the lake as "guy time." Livvy had stayed in the house, putting together the evening's weenie roast and making sure there were enough snacks to get the boys' sugar levels skyrocketing.

Al was the child in the wheelchair, and she marveled at how his brother, the wild and crazy Bo, accepted it and gave him just as much trouble as if he'd been walking.

After Brad had gone back to Obsidian to pick up his wife, the two boys tore around Sunshine, chasing the chicken and enveloping Martha Washington in sticky hugs until she finally retreated under the porch. Leonard simply ran around them all and barked happily.

Finally it was dark enough for fireworks. They could see those being shot off in Medora, the western town on the other side of the butte, but Hayden and Gramps had made sure they had enough of their own, and soon Gramps was lighting the larger fireworks.

The sky lit up as the initial volley of Roman candles exploded into a spectacular display of man-made stars.

Then it was time for the boys to have their own fireworks.

"I want one!"

"I want one, too!"

The excited shouts of Brad's children rang through the night, and Hayden laughed as their little hands greedily clutched at the box of fireworks that he held aloft.

"Remember what your mama said," he told them.

"Don't blow yourselves up!" the children chorused.

"Splendid advice, wouldn't you say?" he answered. "And that extends to parts of yourselves, too. I want to return you both to your parents intact."

"What does that mean?" Bo, the younger child, asked. "What does 'intact' mean?"

"It means with the same number of fingers and toes that you arrived with."

Livvy watched as he distributed the sparklers, spreading them out into exactly equal piles. As one child got green sparklers, so did the other boy.

The box of red sparklers was opened first.

"Light mine first, Uncle Hayden!" The younger child danced around Hayden's legs, slashing the air with the sparkler as if it were a sword.

"No, mine!" Al begged from his wheelchair. "Light mine first. Bo, you wait. You're the baby."

"You're a baby," Bo shot back.

"No, you are."

Livvy interceded. "Neither of you is a baby. You each have a sparkler, and we'll light both of them at exactly the same time."

"Thanks, Aunt Livvy!" the two boys chorused.

She grinned. Everybody was a family member to these boys. Uncle Hayden, Aunt Livvy, Gramps. It was a tremendous feeling.

Soon the children were whooping with glee and mock terror as the sparklers blazed around them. Al certainly wasn't letting being in a wheelchair slow him down. He spun in circles in his chair, waving the sparkler in great loops around him.

"I'm writing *CAT* with mine," Al said. "Aunt Livvy, did you know that we got two cats from here? I call them Tiger and Lion, but Bo calls them Kitty and Cat."

"What do your mom and dad call them?" she asked.

"Mom calls them both Hey You, and Dad calls them Bad and Worse."

Bo whirled happily beside his big brother. "Look, I'm writing my name! Watch me, Uncle Hayden, watch me!"

Hayden leaned close and whispered to her, each word tickling her ear with his closeness. "Good thing his name is Bo and not Archibald. His sparkler wouldn't last!"

She chuckled softly. Hayden was so good with the children, so patient and kind. Together they watched the boys play, enjoying the shouts of laughter and the streaks of color in the night.

Quickly the children lost interest in the sparklers and moved on to colored smoke bombs. Hayden lit them and stepped away, making sure that the boys didn't get too close to the smoking spheres, which looked fascinating but smelled horrible.

The children found them absolutely delightful.

Livvy hung back with Hayden, who began to look a bit green

around the edges as the sulphurous smoke enveloped him.

"That stuff is ghastly," he said, coughing as he moved out of the colorful cloud. "I wonder why they don't scent it or something so it's not so nasty. Bo, too close, too close! Al, no, you're too close, too. It's cool to watch, but the smell—!"

"Maybe you can't have both: looking good and smelling good," she said, wrinkling her nose. The fireworks did stink.

He looked at her, his head tilted to one side. A burst of a Catherine wheel lit his face with silver and blue shots of light. "I think I can."

In the distance, the muted sounds of the pyrotechnics from Medora boomed across the night. She was grateful for the cover of darkness. It hid the flush that had washed over her cheeks.

Was he flirting with her?

The more she thought about it, the more flustered she got. She didn't trust her voice. It would probably squeak or something equally embarrassing.

Instead, she opted for shaking her head.

Her reprieve came in the form of Bo, who ran up to Hayden and tugged on his pant leg. "Uncle Hayden, Uncle Hayden, Uncle Hayden, we blew up all the smoke bombs. What else do you have? Can we blast off one of those big rocket things, please, please, please? I want to light up one of those gigantic things and watch it go zzzzzz through the air!" His pudgy little hands looped in a circle, and Hayden laughed.

"Sorry, buddy, no big rockets for you. Not even little rockets. But I have some snakes."

Bo screamed, "Snakes?" and Livvy smiled to herself. Sunset came so late in summer here, and the children were extremely overtired.

Hayden put a calming hand on Bo's small shoulders. "Not those snakes. These are black chunks that we'll light and then something really cool happens."

Livvy watched as he opened the box and placed the black piece on the concrete slab. He touched a match to what looked like a small dark piece of charcoal and stood back.

"Now watch, and remember, never touch."

The children oohed as the small black nugget began to smolder and expand into a long black curl.

"It kind of smells," the older one confided, pinching his nose shut.

"Good fireworks always smell, don't they, Uncle Hayden?" Bo asked. "Those smoke bombs were really stinkish, too."

"Yes, they do smell. But you know what smells good? S'mores!" Hayden motioned toward the bonfire. "You guys want to make s'mores?"

"Oh, I love them!" Bo shouted enthusiastically, rubbing his hands together in anticipation.

"I like the chocolate." Al wheeled over to Livvy's side and smiled at her. "Can I have double chocolate? You don't have to put the marshmallow on. Or the graham cracker."

She grinned at him. "You just want a candy bar?"

"I think so," he said, "but I'd better cook up a marshmallow just in case."

His eyelids were sagging, and she knew he'd be asleep soon. Bo's energy was getting wilder and wilder, and if her admittedly limited prior experience with children was any indicator, he'd be down for the night within half an hour or so.

The children made it through one and a half s'mores before they had to be carried into the house and put on blankets on the living room floor until their parents arrived. Gramps volunteered to stay with them, and Hayden and Livvy returned to the bonfire, which was beginning to burn low.

Still, sparks shot from the fiery logs, showering the night sky with low stars. She sat next to Hayden, cross-legged. They both smelled of summer, of bug spray, soap, and wood smoke, with a touch of marshmallow and chocolate. It was wonderful. *If Fifth Avenue in New York City could bottle it, they'd make a fortune,* she thought.

Life was good. She was in the middle of one of God's finest creations, the Badlands. A full moon glowed overhead, a shining orb more golden than a treasured coin. Only the crackle of the fire and the calls of the night birds and crickets broke the silence.

She was totally content. The hurriedness of the city—the traffic jams, the crowded sidewalks, the congested stores— seemed as far away as that moon. Nothing mattered except this fire, this moon, this man next to her.

Hayden began to sing softly, a melody that sounded vaguely familiar to her, something she'd heard many years ago. She didn't know the words but she hummed along.

As the last note faded away, she sighed. "That was beautiful."

"It's a Scandinavian hymn that every good child up here learns early on," Hayden said with a low chuckle. "Well, this child learned it. Gramps and Gran made sure of that. We closed every vesper service with it, and it just seemed right tonight to continue the tradition."

"What's the name of it?"

" 'Children of the Heavenly Father.' "

A memory slipped into place. She was sitting at her mother's dressing table, playing with an old music box that she'd used for her earrings.

It was a heavy silver rectangle, inlaid with tiny gold crosses, and it had belonged to her mother's great-aunt Rosalyn, the woman who had taken her mother under her wing when the young girl had lost both her parents in an automobile accident. Livvy had never met her, but she had heard her mother talk about the woman who had dedicated her life to raising a scared eight-year-old girl.

This was the melody that the music box had played. No wonder it sounded familiar.

"Sing it to me again," she asked.

She pulled her knees up close to her, clasping her arms around her legs, and listened as his tenor sweetened the air again with song.

"I know the melody, but I'd never heard the words," she said, and explained about the music box. "That music box has such a history. First it was Mom's great-aunt Rosalyn's repository of her numerous hairpins—my mother always said that the woman left a trail of them wherever she went—and now it holds Mom's earrings. Someday I'll use it. It's the closest thing my family has to an heirloom."

She held up her forefinger. "Wait. That's not quite true, is it? Remember the sermon Reverend Carlisle gave? About the inheritance of faith? Maybe my religious life has been spotty at best, but I'm still in line for the inheritance, too, aren't I?"

This was the ideal place for her to share her heart, between the vast dark sky arching overhead, filled with glittering showers of multicolored lights, and the night-blackened tableau shadowed in the night of the Badlands' epic majesty.

He turned to her, his face illuminated by the still-sparking fire. "You are."

"I want to be part of this." She motioned around her. "I remember when I was in youth group at church—wow, that seems like a long time ago—the leader said that God never forgets us, even if we forget Him. I—I think I have some lost years to make up, when I did forget Him. I hope He remembers me."

"He does. Trust me, He does."

Hayden began to hum "Children of the Heavenly Father" again, and she rested her chin on her knees as she listened. Could ever a night have been more perfect?

The sound of a car turning into the drive heralded the return of the boys' father. Working quickly and quietly, the children were loaded into the vehicle, never waking during the process, and Livvy walked to the truck to drive herself home.

As she pulled away from the house, Hayden waved at her, a silhouette against the last glow of the bonfire.

It had been a lovely Fourth of July. In the distance a lone firework went off, and she smiled as the sound and the light spread across the Badlands.

This was the best Independence Day she'd ever had. Ever.

❧

"I told her that we never locked the door," Gramps said, pacing back and forth as Hayden knelt and examined the situation.

The key had snapped off and was now embedded in the lock.

"It's all right, Gramps," he said. "I'll just get a new one."

Gramps shook his head. "It's the same lock everywhere, Grub. Replace one, replace them all."

"What do you mean?" He rocked back on his heels and looked at his grandfather, who seemed oddly agitated. He spoke slowly, hoping to calm the older man down. "Each lock is different."

Gramps stopped his pacing. "Well, of course they're different. What kind of fool idea would it have been to put locks on all these doors and have the same keys for all those locks? You think I'm a bozo?"

"You're not a bozo. I'm a bozo."

His grandfather shook his head. "Bozo Senior and Bozo Junior. What I mean is that if this key breaks, that means they're all wearing out, and whether we're talking about the keys or the locks, the smartest thing would be to replace them all so this doesn't happen again. Because it will, and you know it will. That's the rule of home ownership. Remember it?"

Hayden grinned at Gramps, and together they recited it. "If it can break, it will break."

"And what's the corollary?" Gramps prompted.

"And it will break in the middle of the night on a weekend."

"That's my boy."

"You're right, Gramps, about these locks. They're all as old as the doors, which are as old as the buildings." Hayden stared at the lock with the key stuck in the hole. If he had to replace all the locks, it would mean—he did a quick mental count—seventeen of them. And assuming each one was as difficult as this one, he'd be doing this until September.

Lord, this would be a great time to dose me with patience, he thought.

The faceplate of the assembly came right off—entirely too easily, he realized, as he examined the door and found that the wood had gone bad under the metal.

The doors would need to be replaced, too.

Dollar signs danced in his head as he performed another

calculation. Seventeen doors. With seventeen locks and seventeen keys.

"Gramps, you'd better get Livvy out here."

The old man scrambled off to get her from behind the house, where she was clearing a bramble-infested patch in the hope that it might be a garden area the next year.

"What's up, doc?" she asked cheerfully, pulling off her pink and yellow work gloves and wiping her hands on her jeans.

"Well, the cost of repairs, that's what's up. This door is rotten under the lock plate. See?" He showed her the damage. "I think we might end up having to replace all the doors and all the lock assemblages."

She frowned. "That's a lot."

"I'm afraid it is."

"I have my book. I think it might explain how to do it."

He shook his head. She wasn't understanding what he meant. "Livvy, I'm afraid we're going to have to buy new doors."

She crossed her arms over her chest and frowned. "Wow."

"Definitely wow. So what should we do?"

She shrugged. "There's no point in borrowing trouble. Let's take a look at the other doors. Maybe they don't all need to be replaced. And if they do, then I guess we need to go somewhere and buy a truckload of doors. And locks."

"Good idea," he agreed.

They walked around the property, checking each door, and he was relieved to discover that the cabins and outbuildings that faced east had no damage. It was only those that faced into the wind that came off the Badlands that needed help.

"That's good." She smiled happily, pulling her work gloves back on.

"Well, it's better. There are still quite a lot of them."

"Oh!" She stopped and clapped one hand, still in the silly pink and yellow flowered cotton glove, over her mouth. "I see. Well, I have the book. I can do it. How hard can it be?"

Those were, he knew from experience, famous last words. The sun was setting by the time he'd gotten back from the building supply store in Bismarck, and she'd gotten one latch replaced, and the door at least leaned against its building.

"Tomorrow is another day," she said, "and another door, and by the time I finish it'll be another year."

He laughed. It wasn't that bad. Not quite.

&

Livvy wiped her forehead. The heat was relentless. She felt as if she were living inside an oven. The only breeze that came through was the occasional hot wind off the buttes, and it didn't improve her temperament one bit.

If this was July, she could only imagine what August would be like.

The doors were done. At least that was taken care of. Now she was doing her least favorite thing in the world: cleaning.

She made a deal with herself. If she could finish scrubbing out the cabin, she would take a break and go wading in the lake. There wasn't too much to do, just some work on the sills and prying the accumulated crud out of the corners of the mopboards.

She took a swig out of the water bottle she kept on the little table shoved up against the window. The ice in it had long since melted, and the water was very warm.

The windows were flung open, but the air inside the cabin was still and motionless. Sweat rolled down her face and dripped onto her T-shirt. She tried to think of pleasant things—mountaintops covered in snow, ice skating, making snowballs—but her mind kept reverting to the same phrase: "I'm hot."

In self-defense, she wrenched open the bottle of water and poured it over her head. For a few moments, it actually helped. She felt a smidge cooler.

She knelt and tackled a corner of the room, digging away at the stuff that had built up in there. "One day," she said through gritted teeth, "someone, probably a woman, will get smart and make a room without corners so no other human being will ever have to do this again."

"A round house isn't impossible," Hayden said from the doorway, "but it's a lot of extra work to build."

She swabbed her face with the back of her hand. "Typical man," she said. "Worrying about a few extra minutes of work."

He laughed. "We'll not fight that one out today. I thought you might be broiling in here, so I brought you this."

He held out a large plastic mug with a straw sticking out of it. "It might be a bit melted but I kept the AC on full blast on my way back from Obsidian so it would have a chance."

She took it from him and practically inhaled the contents. "Oh, this is heavenly. I haven't had a root beer float for ages."

"Yup. I got it from the drive-through on the edge of town. Take a break. You look like you could use one."

Livvy laughed. "Thanks for the compliment—not!"

"You're always beautiful," Hayden answered, and almost immediately he flushed bright red. "I mean, well, when you're clean, or not, but then, actually, um. . ."

He looked so miserable, stammering in the heat in front of her, that she took pity on him. "Thanks, Hayden. Beauty is as beauty does, and this is a mighty beautiful root beer float!"

seven

"Shoo! Shoo! Go find a hollow tree, or wherever it is you live!" Livvy swept the chubby raccoon out of the lean-to near the house where she was stacking firewood. Indian summer was in full swing this October day. She was sweating, and having to get wildlife out of the building wasn't improving her mood one bit.

The raccoon waddled away as quickly as it could, stopping for one last snarl before vanishing into the woods, and she leaned on the woodpile, feeling for all the world like a Wild West woman.

Every day she went through cardboard boxes, plastic containers, and wooden crates. Most of it was disposed of immediately. She had learned to recognize when mice—or raccoons—had been in containers. Unfortunately they were destructive creatures, and almost everything they'd gotten into was taken to the dump.

Some of it was interesting, especially the memorabilia from Sunshine's heyday. That she put aside. Hayden and Gramps could go through it during the winter and see what they wanted to keep and which pictures they could identify. She hoped they'd let her keep some of it at Sunshine to use as a reminder of its past.

And some was sad, like Gran's clothing, which Gramps had put aside when she passed away. He'd been unable to take care of it, and unwilling to let someone else do it for him.

Now, with his permission, her clothing had gone to a charity.

There was just so much of everything.

She was trying to get each outbuilding finished before the snow came. Hayden had warned her that the first measurable snow could fall any day now, even if the days were still in the fifties and sixties, although today had climbed into the seventies. The forecast predicted a drop the next day, with the evening temperatures plummeting to the thirties, and the next week the first hard freeze was a possibility. At night, she thought she could smell snow in the distance.

Hayden and Gramps were sharing Hayden's apartment in Obsidian, and she'd moved to Sunshine with Leonard. Jeannie had decided that she wasn't coming back from Africa—her house had been sold to a young couple in town—and suddenly Livvy had become a dog owner. It was fine with her. Leonard kept her company, and she felt safer at night when the land became alive with sounds she couldn't identify.

So much had changed. She'd never been really overweight, but the labor had built up her muscles and tightened her frame. Now she could lift a box without having to empty half of it first, or call upon Hayden or whoever was handy to help her out. Her skin was tanned—naturally, without benefit of a tanning bed or a spray or a lotion.

She glanced at her arm. Not only was it tan, it was scratched from a recent run-in with the chicken that had tried to peck a bug off of Martha Washington's back. The cat had tangled with the chicken, and when she tried to separate them, they'd both clawed her.

And next to those scratches were two cuts from a run-in with a broken window, and a bruise that came about when an old radio had fallen from a high shelf and she'd foolishly tried to catch it.

She shook her head as she thought back to that morning in Boston, when a stray newspaper had changed her life. She was no longer the same person she was that day.

But the greatest changes were internal. As much as she'd always considered herself to be independent and self-sufficient, she knew now how dependent she'd been on others. If her car needed an oil change, she took it in to a mechanic.

Now she knew how to do it herself—and she did it. Plus, with her initial plumbing adventure behind her, she was able to change washers in a faucet and reseat a leaking toilet.

She began to tally what she knew now that she hadn't known before.

She could replace a light switch. Change breakers. Even bait her own hook—with a worm.

Her confidence was stronger than it had ever been before.

As much as Sunshine was responsible for this newfound strength, she knew that the majority of credit went to the peace and guidance she'd found in the church. Every week she came away from the services knowing herself better. She was truly a child of God, and just knowing that had made her feel like a new, improved Livvy.

Every evening she set aside time for her own private vespers. With her Bible at hand, she'd read and then study the passages, using the guides that Reverend Carlisle had lent her. Even though she had watched programs on the Travel Channel about Israel, it still seemed alien to her, but with this reading, she was able to get a better sense of the historical context.

What was most important though was that she was able to bridge those years, two thousand of them, and take the lessons of the past and bring them into the present day, and use them to guide her through the time yet to come.

She especially though found understanding through prayer. Talking to God helped her clarify what her life was about, and more importantly, what it could be about.

If she could only get the cloud of the future to quit hanging over her head, she'd feel much better. It still kept her up at night, tossing and turning, with sleep eluding her. She prayed and prayed her way through those wide-awake hours, asking for an answer, for a solution.

What was she going to do? That question had to be answered, and soon. She'd checked her bank balance online and was horrified to see how much it had shrunk.

She'd been hasty in packing up and moving to North Dakota. There was no doubt about that. But she could not believe it had been the wrong thing to do. Never.

Sunshine was in her soul. As the summer had moved into autumn, it had become even more enmeshed in her being.

God clearly meant for her to be there. Didn't He? If it was His intent, was He at some time going to make clear to her what she should do? Something that would be profitable?

It was too much to ask of Him. She knew that. She'd gone into this with her eyes wide open—maybe with a bit of a shadow from her fashionable sunglasses that Leonard had gnawed into a twisted, unusable piece of plastic, but open nonetheless.

She wouldn't trade back an hour of all the work she'd done for even a second of time back in her very comfortable office with the padded leather chair and the checks that made life tolerable. No, she was glad to be here, in the last shreds of warmth before winter set in.

But there was just so much to be done at Sunshine.

She'd spent so much time focusing on cleaning and repairing the buildings that she'd let her original vision for it fall aside. Now, as she was about to enter her first winter here in North Dakota, she'd have the time to work on developing it.

She had only the vaguest idea of what she wanted to do with the property. A fishing resort was the only thing she'd come up with, but that was so nebulous, it was worthless.

Initially Sunshine had appealed to her because of how different it was from the hustle of the city. Then she had met Hayden and Gramps, and the mission became different—it was no longer saving her sanity, but saving Sunshine.

And saving her soul.

Suddenly a volley of sharp barks erupted from Leonard, who, from his vantage point on the porch, had been happily watching Hayden paint the front door. The dog tore down the driveway, and continued to bark at whatever unseen menace was headed their way.

Livvy pulled off her work gloves and stepped out of the lean-to. A cloud of dust announced visitors.

It was Trevor's old truck. This was the vehicle that had brought her to Sunshine in the first place, and she started for it, a smile on her face, when the passenger side door opened, and a familiar figure stepped out.

It couldn't be. It just couldn't be.

She moved toward the truck, but Hayden was faster, reaching it before she did. Leonard growled at the stranger and protectively placed himself firmly between the man and Hayden.

"Good dog, Leonard, good dog." Hayden patted the dog's head with one hand while keeping a firm grip on his collar with the other. "Settle down now. Good dog, good dog. By the way," he said to the visitor, "I'm Hayden Greenwood."

"Pleased to meet you," the man answered, his dark eyes sweeping across the property. "I'm—"

In a split second, as she saw the familiar scan—the rapid tally, the quick appraisal of market value—a protective temper rose in her. Sunshine was hers.

She knew from working with the man that he did nothing without a firm objective in mind. What did he want from her? It couldn't be good.

Livvy stepped forward. "This is Michael Evans, my former boss."

Hayden turned to her, clearly startled by her blunt tone. "Livvy—" he began, but she waved his interruption away, and Mr. Evans laughed a bit nervously as Leonard growled again.

"Mr. Evans is here to see me, or, no, better than that, I'm wondering if he's here to see Sunshine," she said, hating that her voice was shaking. "What is it? Is there oil under the land? Gold tucked in a cave? Gemstones in the buttes?"

She tried to interject some lightness into her words, but she knew she failed. She knew him too well. He wasn't here because he was on vacation in the Badlands. Not Michael Evans. Their relationship in Boston had been very formal, very careful, very precise. Their parting hadn't been exactly cordial either.

There was some reason he was here, and it had to do with Sunshine. Or her.

He had some kind of agenda, and the most effective way to deal with it was to face it head-on, directly.

Mr. Evans looked at her, and she saw herself in his eyes. Cut-off jeans, a faded and stained T-shirt that she'd found in one of the cabins a month ago, no makeup, and hair that hadn't seen a stylist since she left Boston. To complete the package, she probably smelled like dirt and sweat and was coated in both.

"Actually," he said, his voice as smooth as Martha Washington's fur, "I'm out here because I need your signature on some papers."

"Really?" she asked, making no effort to disguise the disbelief in her voice. "And what papers would those be?"

"The Millner transfer. You didn't sign the agent's agreement."

Livvy shook her head in self-reproach. She knew exactly what he was talking about. She'd done all of the behind-the-scenes work on the account. It had been a massive amount of work because the Millners owned rental property not only in Massachusetts but also in Virginia, Florida, and Arizona. Each state's laws were a bit different, and adding to the difficulty was that the Millner family, which was spread all around the world, owned varying percentages of each property. It was the largest account she'd ever worked with. She'd left before everything was completed—the finalization had still been months away.

And yet of all the papers for her to miss, the agreement was probably the most important.

"You don't get your bonus until it's signed," Mr. Evans said, knowing, she was sure, that those very words would make her get out her pen immediately.

She'd forgotten about the bonus. It was a substantial one. With it, she'd be able to get through the winter—if nothing broke.

She took a moment and breathed a prayer: *Give me patience, strength, and understanding.*

"I apologize if I sounded rude," she said, motioning him to the door. "Come inside, and let's put ink on paper."

Gramps was at the screen door. "All that commotion woke me up from my nap," he said. His eyes were confused. "Is Ellie in the garden?"

She took his arm. "Hayden is right out here. And we have a guest, Gramps. This is Michael Evans. I worked for him in Boston. He owns one of the largest real estate management firms in the United States."

Mr. Evans reached his hand out and shook Gramps's. "Sir, it's good to meet you. This is my first time in North Dakota, and I must say it's quite a spectacular place. Sunshine has a beautiful setting."

Gramps nodded. "Sunshine is a treasure." He shook his arm free of his touch. "You can't have it."

She bit back a smile at her former boss's expression. He managed to look horrified and amused at the same time. He had clearly underestimated Gramps's mental facility, which didn't surprise her too much. He'd always sent her to negotiate with family members.

What he didn't know—had never known—was the reason she was so successful with estate work. She didn't push the family members but instead guided them to a consensus, one that they could all be happy with.

"I don't want Sunshine," Mr. Evans said in the voice he usually kept in reserve for those he considered slow.

"Then you're dumber than I thought." Gramps pulled the screen door shut and hooked the latch.

She heard Hayden gasp behind her, and in a series of great

loping steps, he joined them. "Gramps, now, Mr. Evans is here to visit with Livvy. He has something she needs to sign."

The old man shook his head vigorously. "He's here to sell something. Vacuum cleaners maybe. Or toilet brushes."

A nervous giggle rose in her throat, but she choked it down. Gramps's fingers tapped nervously along the handle of the door.

"I can assure you, sir," Mr. Evans said, "that I am not here to sell anything, especially not vacuum cleaners or toilet brushes." He said the products as if the very words tasted bad.

Livvy glanced quickly at Hayden. His forehead was lined with worry. He reached toward the door but Gramps shook his head, and Hayden shoved his hands into his jeans pockets and looked upward, his face a study in frustration.

A loud rumble accompanied by blares and screeches rose behind them, and Livvy spun around to see the cause.

It was Trevor. Apparently bored by the entire scene, he'd started his car again—those were the sounds that shook the floorboards of the porch—and turned on the radio. It might have been music that he was listening to, but Livvy wouldn't stake any bets on it.

"Is that Martha Washington?" Gramps asked, and from somewhere deep inside Livvy, a bubble of laughter burst and erupted out of her. Hayden looked at her, and he joined in, too.

Mr. Evans gaped at them as if they'd both lost their minds, and as the laughter continued to pour out into the October afternoon, unchecked, she thought that perhaps he was right. She could no more stop laughing than she could sprout wings and fly around the yard.

She reached for Hayden and put her hand on his shoulder to balance herself as the laughter rolled on. It felt so good to laugh. It cleaned her. It refreshed her. And it gave her new vigor.

At last Mr. Evans coughed, a sound that shot through the growl of Trevor's truck engine and the shrill blast of guitars and drums and wailing voices from his radio, and the last vestiges of mirth died in her throat.

"Can you explain this to me?" he asked rather stiffly. "I am somewhat at a disadvantage here."

"Martha Washington is a cat," she answered, wiping her eyes from the laughing jag. "A big fat lazy cat that chases the chicken and that's about all. She purrs but not quite that loudly."

Gramps wiggled the screen door. "It's locked," he announced.

Hayden cleared his throat and approached the door. "Gramps, you locked it."

"I know."

"Now you need to unlock it."

The older man fiddled with the latch and at last it sprang free.

Hayden opened the door and motioned Livvy and Mr. Evans inside.

She took her former boss into the kitchen as Hayden led his grandfather to the couch and began to talk to him in a low voice.

Mr. Evans looked over his shoulder. "He's all right?"

Livvy nodded. "He fades in and out. Usually he's fine. He's the fellow I bought Sunshine from."

"I see."

As they neared the table, he opened the large manila folder he carried and took out the papers, looking through them, not losing a step in his stride. "I would have done this by phone, but I couldn't get through."

"No service right here. At least not for that carrier."

"And then you weren't answering your e-mail," he continued.

"No Internet out here."

Mr. Evans stopped midstep. "You're serious? No cell phone service. No e-mail. No Google."

"I'm serious. The only thing I miss is talking to my parents, since they live in Sweden, and we use the computer for that, so I go into town and use the library's connection."

He stared at her. "Amazing." He laid the papers on the scarred surface of the kitchen table and ran his hands over the faux marble top. "This would get a fairly decent price at auction, wouldn't it? Now let's see, Release, Assignment of Rights, Temporary Transfer of Title, Deed in Kind, Agent's Agreement, there we are. You have a pen? Sign by the yellow sticky note."

He seemed anxious to move the conversation on, to get out of the kitchen of this place where crazies lived, and she didn't totally blame him. She read through the document, making sure that she remembered what she had written before she signed it. It was a good agreement, fair to all those involved, but it had involved months of work, of close negotiation, of listening, listening, and more listening.

She was justifiably proud of what she'd accomplished, and she signed it with a tinge of sadness, knowing that she would probably never do this kind of work again. There weren't enough property sales or leases to make her career possible out here.

"Here you go," she said, blowing on the inked signature before handing it back to him. Mr. Evans always used a fountain pen that she knew cost several hundreds of dollars. "Signed, sort of sealed, and delivered."

"Thank you." He placed the document back in the folder and snapped the rubber band around it. "This means a lot to the agency, and, of course, to you. You deserved this bonus. I'm not one to give out compliments, you know that, but the clients have told me repeatedly how much they appreciated what you did for them. Thanks to you, the family has reunited, despite the friction of the past, and they asked me to relay their appreciation to you for your work, not just as an agent but as a human being."

She could only stare at him. This was amazing.

"Do you have a card?" he asked.

"What kind of a card?" She looked at him blankly.

"A business card," he answered, "of course."

"Business card? For what?"

"Well, for one thing, to make sure the check arrives here, unless you want it automatically deposited in the bank. Do you still have the same account?"

"I do." For once her laziness was in her favor. She'd left the account in Boston open. "Can you go ahead and deposit it for me?"

"Sure. But you should have a business card."

"Why?"

He put the packet flat onto the table. "Well, Livvy, for this." He motioned around him with a sweep of his arm. "Sunshine. You can't do this without advertising. It's the stuff of business success, after all. You'll need to start the accounts for food service, unless you want to do it all yourself, and there'll be a cleaning crew, I imagine, and a linen supply contract, just to begin."

"But for what?" She understood the words but there wasn't meaning behind them. What on earth was he talking about?

A fly roused itself on the windowsill and batted itself halfheartedly against the screen, warmed by the Indian summer afternoon. Outside the cacophony of Trevor's truck radio and engine shook the usual calm.

"For this." He leaned on the table, his black suit still spotless even after riding in the teenager's truck. She'd been in the truck just five months ago, and she doubted that he had cleaned it since. How Mr. Evans accomplished maintaining his immaculate appearance was nothing short of a miracle.

She could only shake her head.

He sat down, keeping his back stick-straight, crossed his legs, and looked her directly in the eye. "For when you reopen. You are reopening, aren't you?"

She knew Michael Evans well enough to pay attention when he was positioned like this, poised and attentive. She used to say that she could see his ears literally perk up when he sensed a business opportunity. She let him continue speaking, anxious to let him share his vision.

"This would be a splendid resort," he said.

"But it wasn't working," she objected, pretending that she hadn't been thinking of just that. The more she could learn from this man's years of cagey expertise, the better. "Plus it's not exactly Hawaii or the Riviera."

"The destination is what you create." He looked out the window, and Livvy's eyes followed his. The copper and bronze of the Badlands were framed against the bright blue of the sky. "Look at that. You name me one other place that has that. And I wager that if that teenager would turn off his truck, we'd hear only nature. Am I right?"

She nodded, beginning to feel a twinge of excitement.

"Figure out what kind of resort you'd like it to be." He stood and picked up the folder and tucked it under his arm. "I'd make it a retro theme, and market it to L.A. and New York. Big Internet splash, which is practically free. I bet that kid out there could cobble up a webpage with his eyes closed. Run off some flyers on a printer, nice full-color images with this place all spiffed up, and blast them to travel agents out there."

It sounded wonderful, and as she listened, the ideas started to take root.

"One question, Mr. Evans," she said as she walked him to the truck, nearly shouting to be heard over the music coming from Trevor's radio. "Why aren't you trying to get this from me, open it yourself, if it's such a great business proposition?"

"Me?" he asked. He opened the door of the truck and with a look of complete revulsion, flicked a bug off the seat and climbed into the cab. He placed the packet neatly centered on his knees and snapped the safety belt across his shoulders. Then he faced her squarely, and with a voice just a touch under the decibels still thundering from the radio, said, "I don't want it. But you do, and that's what counts. You have heart, Miss Moore, and that's what this is going to take. North Dakota heart."

Trevor caught her eye over Mr. Evans's shoulder and grinned, making loopy "crazy" signs and pointing at the real estate magnate.

She smiled back.

She loved this place, loved this old house, even loved this obnoxious truck and its driver and its blaring radio and amped-up engine.

North Dakota heart, indeed!

❧

The chill of autumn was definitely in the air. That Indian summer day had passed, and the temperatures had become more October-like. The leaves on the trees along the river began to dry, and when the afternoon winds picked up, they rattled together like shells, a wind chime heralding the end of summer and the time-to-come of winter.

The little apartment in Obsidian was cozy—which was a code word for *cramped*. Gramps was still with him awaiting an opening in the senior living facility, and while Hayden was grateful to have his grandfather with him, a one-bedroom apartment was just that—one bedroom. He'd given Gramps the bed, and he'd been bunking on the couch in the living room, which was about ten inches too short for any comfort.

He sat at the kitchen table, papers that needed to be graded spread out in front of him, but he wasn't seeing them. Too much was on his mind to be able to focus on the area of a trapezoid if side D was 1.3 and side B was 2.4.

Livvy had moved out to Sunshine, and they had an awkward arrangement. He'd bring Gramps out to her during the day, and he'd come back to Obsidian and teach. Then, at the end of the school day, he'd return to Sunshine, visit with Livvy and make sure everything was working well, and retrieve Gramps and the two of them would drive to Obsidian, to the tiny apartment.

He felt better knowing that Gramps was not alone during the day, but it was asking a lot of Livvy to have the older man out there all day long. And as the season progressed, he wasn't sure it would continue to work.

But it had to. There just wasn't any choice. Some things

had to be the way they were, and that was simply all there was to it.

Gramps was in the living room, watching a video of an Elvis Presley movie he'd gotten at the grocery store. Why he'd chosen it from the rack of movie rentals, Hayden had no idea, but the old man had seemed delighted with the choice and was now deeply engrossed in it.

He stacked the homework into a neat pile and laid it aside. Maybe later he could get to it, but first he had to deal with what was topmost in his mind.

He picked up the envelope and removed the sheet of paper and read it once again. What should he do?

He buried his face in his hands in a futile attempt to wipe out what was in front of him. He had taken action, and now—now did he want it?

Earlier in the year, on a February day when the high was five below zero and the winds would not stop, he impetuously applied for a teaching job in Florida. He spread his fingers a tad and peeked through the opening at the correspondence in front of him. There were the letters, forming the words and sentences he had wanted to hear, and now dreaded. They had an opening and needed him to teach: Could he come for an interview?

He couldn't leave. Sunshine might be sold, but his grandfather needed him. And without a place for Gramps to live, he had to stay in Obsidian. Until a spot opened in the senior living complex, his grandfather would have to live with him.

Not that he minded. He would walk over hot coals and through burning lava for his grandfather.

Plus there was Livvy. Livvy with her cap of dark hair that

curled wildly when it rained, with her eyes so deeply brown that they glowed. She needed him to help her with Sunshine. There was no way she could do it by herself, not with just that goofy book to help her. What was the name of it again? Oh yes. *The Complete Guide to Home Construction and Repair.*

He put his hands together, palm to palm. When he had been a little boy, that's what he would do when he prayed. He tried it now, asking for clarity, for comfort, for reassurance.

Usually he got a pleasant, warm feeling from his prayers, a sense that they had been heard and acknowledged, and this was no different. He came away from his brief time with the Lord refreshed and ready to face what was ahead.

Sadly, what was ahead was a stack of ungraded math worksheets.

He took a deep breath and dug in. Right now his problems were mathematical. The rest of them would have to wait.

❧

"We need a bonfire," Gramps announced one Saturday afternoon, when the three of them were at Sunshine. "One more bonfire before winter hits."

They had just finished painting the interior of one of the old cabins, and they were sitting on the porch, enjoying the notion that there was just one more cabin to refinish before they would have all been renovated. It was a pleasant feeling.

Martha Washington grunted in her sleep. She was curled on Gramps's lap in a furry ball. At the sound, one of Leonard's ears perked up, but he didn't open his eyes, apparently deeming a cat snort to be unimportant.

Livvy didn't want to move. She wanted to sit in the chair with the slatted back and absorb the last rays of the weekend sun, wrapped in the soft fleece of a blanket.

Only one cabin was left. It seemed like it had been a race against the calendar, fixing one or two cabins a week so they'd be ready for visitors in the spring. If the weather held, she could probably get the last one done in the coming week, and maybe even get the old canteen painted. She'd found another box of the old signs. They'd be perfect in there.

She shut her eyes and let her imagination roam. A clear light blue, one that matched the summer sky here in North Dakota, would be perfect for the walls. She'd leave the signs as she'd found them, a few rusted, some partially broken, others in pristine shape, and scatter them across the walls.

Café curtains would let the sun in but filter the brightness. Maybe she could find some old-fashioned chintz, with the same color of blue as the walls, and perhaps a retro theme of families enjoying themselves on the water. She'd seen something like that at one time in Boston, back in a store that specialized in old-fashioned fabric themes. They probably would send her what she needed, if she could find samples on the Internet.

The Internet. She was connected again, thanks to the wonders of technology, and life was good. A satellite dish was tastefully positioned on the far side of the house, and through some marvels she didn't understand, she had Internet, cell phone reception, and even more television channels than she could ever watch. Coverage didn't extend beyond the house, but that was all right.

Now she wouldn't have to drive into town to check her bank balances. She'd been spending her evenings investigating what kind of flowers she could plant around the house, and maybe she'd have a vegetable patch for fresh corn and tomatoes. She'd have to ask Hayden about that.

"We could," Hayden said from the porch swing next to her. "What do you say, Livvy?"

She forced her eyes open. "About what?"

"About a bonfire."

"Tonight?"

"Sure."

"Would I have to move? Or can I stay right here and you do all the work?" She closed her eyes again. There really was nothing like the late autumn sun.

Martha Washington had it right. Sleep on the porch in the afternoon. Sit back, and relax. There would be time for work—well, for her anyway. Martha's days of working were long over. She was now replaced by traps in the outbuildings, and it didn't seem to bother her at all.

"Sure. All we have to do is put more wood on the pile and put a match to it. You've got marshmallows, right?"

She nodded, not bothering to raise her eyelids. "Amazingly, I do. I was going to make cereal bars with them but that would require me to move, and that's not going to happen."

"Do you have hot dogs?"

"Nope."

"What do you think, Gramps? Should we go back into town and get some?"

The old man's chair creaked as he rocked. Apparently the motion didn't bother the cat; Livvy could hear her snoring continue uninterrupted.

"I put some pork chops in the Crock-Pot this morning," Gramps said, "so we've got them for dinner. Let's just go with the marshmallows. But you'll need to go get some more logs, Grub. Down by the river, on the north edge, I think I saw some trees that didn't make it through this last season.

They'll be fine for a bonfire."

"Probably too smoky, I'd say," Hayden commented.

"Smoky is okay. We're outside. And it'll keep the bugs away."

"I'd rather use seasoned wood. There's a pile over by the orange cabin."

She could hear the teasing in his voice, and his grandfather rose to the occasion. "That's good lumber. That's not the stuff you burn. You might as well throw this chair onto the fire. Or that porch post. Maybe the kitchen table. . ."

Livvy let the sound of their good-natured repartee wash over her like a lullaby, a backdrop to the soft chatter of the dried leaves that still clung to the trees, and the faint splash of the river, and the distant calls of birds that still lingered before migrating south. Wrapped in a blanket in the cool evening, she was so comfortable. Who knew that this would be one of life's greatest pleasures, relaxing outside at the edge of winter? She knew she was falling asleep, but something kept nudging her arm.

"Leonard, go away," she muttered drowsily. "I don't want to throw the ball."

"You don't have to throw the ball. You just have to come in and have a pork chop." It was Hayden's voice. "Gramps got the table all set, and there's a nice salad, and he's got some goopy stuff he puts on the meat that makes it heavenly."

"What?" She sat up and rubbed her eyes, still groggy.

"I don't know exactly what it is, but it's really good. You'd better come in and try it. His pork chops are almost as good as his peanut butter and jelly sandwiches."

"Was I asleep?" she asked. "I was just listening to you and Gramps talk about the wood, and—"

"And you were gone."

She could feel the red rushing to her face. "Oh please tell me I wasn't snoring."

"Okay, you weren't snoring." He grinned.

"I was, wasn't I?"

"Maybe a little bit."

"You and Martha Washington had a regular concerto going," Gramps said from behind the screen door.

"Oh my. Oh my." She hurried to her feet. "I'm so sorry. I know I can get going sometimes, but to do it in public! I'm so embarrassed!"

Hayden smiled. "I don't know that Gramps and I really qualify as the public, but let me reassure you that it was a very ladylike little sound, just breathing with enthusiasm, actually."

"Baloney. She was sawing logs like a lumberjack," Gramps said, shaking his head. "I like that in a woman."

"You like to hear a woman snoring?" She gaped at him.

"Sure," the older man responded, holding the screen door open for her. "It shows she's no delicate hothouse flower."

"Well, I'm definitely not that," she answered, following the men into the kitchen, where the most delicious aroma in the world was wafting from. "But on the other hand, I've never been compared to a lumberjack before either."

The dinner was astonishing, and when she said as much, Gramps simply shrugged. "It's the Crock-Pot. You put a lot of interesting things in there, and the Crock-Pot takes it from there."

After they ate, the men dismissed themselves to build the bonfire. As she cleared the table and loaded the dishwasher, their voices floated through the open window over the sink.

"Big logs on the bottom now," Gramps coached, "and remember to put the twigs under the logs, that's right, but leave some sticking out so they can catch fire."

"I know, Gramps."

"I'm just reminding you, Grub. We don't want to get your lady friend out here and then have a dud of a fire."

"She's not my lady friend."

"Not yet. All you have to do though is make your move and she's yours."

"She's not mine."

The conversation had taken a fascinating turn, and Livvy put down the dish towel and eavesdropped shamelessly.

"She likes you. I can see it in the way she looks at you, and her eyes and your eyes hold, just a bit longer than most, and her face softens, and she leans toward you until you're almost touching but you're not, and—"

"Oh Gramps. You're just being silly now."

"I'm not. Your grandmother knew."

"She knew about Livvy?"

"Sure."

A sudden silence fell over the evening. Only a night bird coo-hoo'ed in the distance.

Then Hayden spoke, slowly and clearly. "Gramps, Gran is in heaven."

"I know that," the old man said. "You think I don't know that? You think I don't miss her every single waking minute? You think that sometimes it might not make me happy to think of her? And you know what? You know what? We were together for so long that I know how she thought, and what she'd say today. After you've loved someone for that long, you know. You just know."

"Gramps, I'm sorry—" Hayden began, but his grandfather interrupted him.

"You know I don't usually talk to you like this, but I know you're worried about me because I get mixed up. I do. I admit it. When you've had as many days as I've had, they sometimes run into each other and get blurry. I see blurry. I hear blurry. And I think blurry. But I do know that your grandmother isn't with me. I know that."

Something wet fell onto Livvy's hand, and she realized she was crying.

Hayden murmured something indistinct.

Gramps continued, "She did say something about Livvy. She didn't know her, of course, but she knew that Livvy was coming into your life. She told me the day she died, Grub, that there was a woman for you, someone who would love you and treasure you for all of your days, who would be there when you needed her—and when you didn't. And that she would be a child of God, just as you are. She was telling the truth. She was. That woman is Livvy."

"I know." The two words carried across the yard, through the window, and into Livvy's heart.

"And you should—Leonard, drop that stick! No, bad dog! No! Grub, do you see what that dim-witted beast is doing to our woodpile? Stop, you dumb dog!"

She grinned as the big dog crashed into the carefully piled stack of wood and kindling, digging into it with his big feet and flinging aside branch after branch.

Hayden struggled to nab Leonard, but the dog, seeing this as a grand adventure, eluded his grip, while Gramps stood on the sidelines, stamping his feet in the old patched boots and yelling at the dog.

She sniffed back the last vestiges of tears, and joined them. "Leonard baby, come to Mama," she cooed, and the dog dropped the great stick he had in his mouth and trotted over to see her.

"Leonard baby, come to Mama?" Hayden repeated. "Leonard baby, come to Mama?"

She sank to the ground and hugged the mutt. "He just wanted some attention, didn't you, sweetie?"

Out of the corner of her eye, she saw the two men exchange looks and shake their heads, and she buried her smile in the dog's fur. "All's well that ends well, right, Leonard?" she murmured in his ear. "You are a crazy creature though."

Hayden and Gramps rebuilt the stack for the bonfire as the dog, happy now, went off to the porch where he chased the chicken off the padded chair and sprawled across it himself. Martha Washington ignored the entire fracas.

Sunset came earlier than it had in the summer when the days seemed to last forever. Now they arrived quickly, and the land was covered in shadows that stretched from the buttes to the mesas to the flatlands.

Hayden lit the bonfire, and soon the entire pile of wood was ablaze. Sparks crackled upward into the darkness, and the four of them—Livvy, Hayden, Gramps, and Leonard— circled around the flames. Hayden distributed sticks and they stuck marshmallows on and let them roast until they caught fire.

"This is the best way," Livvy said, pulling her marshmallow from the fire and blowing it out. "Good and crispy and totally charred."

She waved it around until it was cool enough and gave it

to Leonard, who consumed it in a single gulp, and then she roasted another one for herself.

A stray ember popped onto Leonard's paw, and he ran back to the safety of the porch. Soon Gramps yawned broadly. "This old body needs some sleep. I want to be rested for church tomorrow. Livvy, you don't mind if I bunk for a while on the couch, do you? Grub, just wake me up before you leave."

Livvy waved and watched as he headed for the house with his odd gait.

Neither she nor Hayden spoke. Only the *snap* of the logs in the fire and the sounds of the night birds disturbed the stillness. She put the bag of marshmallows aside. If she ate any more, she'd look like a marshmallow herself soon.

She didn't want to think about the conversation she had overheard between Hayden and Gramps, but it insisted, making its way into her brain.

Maybe she had misunderstood what Hayden had said. Maybe he didn't feel as strongly about her as he'd implied. After all, he hadn't even kissed her. As a matter of fact, he hadn't shown any sign that he even wanted to.

And didn't that matter?

It did to her. She hadn't let herself think about Hayden as somebody she could love, but now—now it seemed that she had skipped that part entirely and had gone straight to being in love.

The words settled into her brain.

She loved Hayden.

And now, more than anything, she wanted him to kiss her.

She looked at him. His face, lit in profile by the amber and gold flames, was that of a kind and caring man. He turned and looked at her, and they moved toward each other, knowing that they were meant to be together, meant to kiss.

So many times she'd kissed and then thought herself in love. This way though—it was perfect.

It seemed as if the world moved in slow motion, as he leaned toward her and she toward him. It was going to happen. He was going to kiss her.

Could anything be more filled with a sense of the future than the moments between the decision to kiss, and the kiss itself? The air was charged with expectation and electricity. . . and hope.

At last, when she didn't think she could bear it a second longer, their lips touched. It was a sacred time. An unspoken promise passed between them, a promise of love that had always existed, and of love that would grow to the ends of the universe. It was a promise of a commitment to a love that would hold them both to the standard of a God that loved them both, and by His love, gave them a model of how they should love each other.

"Livvy," Hayden said at last, "I love you."

"You sound surprised," she said, her voice shaking with new emotion.

In the flickering light of the bonfire, his face creased into an uneasy frown. "I shouldn't have said that."

She inhaled sharply. This was not what she wanted to hear. "Why not?"

"Well," he said, reaching up and brushing a strand of hair from her forehead, "I should have waited to say that. It was too soon. I know how it's supposed to go. We're supposed to date, and then after a couple of dates, we'd kiss, and then months later, I'd say I loved you."

"Why?" She paused for a moment. "I think your timing was perfect. Hayden, I think, I mean, I'm pretty sure, yes, I am positive that I love you, too."

He laughed. "We sound like we're first-timers at this love thing."

"Honestly, I am. I can't say that I ever was in love before this." She thought back to her prom dates, to crushes she'd had during college, and the few bad dates she'd had in Boston, mostly ill-conceived business meetings disguised as social encounters.

"Well," he said, "if we need some guides, I've got 122 high school students who are all convinced that they know what love is all about and who would be glad to advise us."

She leaned her head on his shoulder. The faint scent of shaving cream mingled with the woodsy aroma of the bonfire, and she thought she had never smelled anything quite so good.

So this was love. It was the sweetest emotion she'd ever felt.

He slid his arm around her and held her closely. He felt so sturdy, so solid, so dependable.

For the past four months, she'd relied on him for his help with renovating Sunshine, and every single day, he had been there for her, helping her with the antiquated plumbing, replacing worn window fittings, painting, cleaning, and sorting through boxes.

Not once had he complained.

He'd not only fixed up Sunshine; he helped mend her soul. He guided her back to her position as a child of God, and while she was still learning, that fact alone had brought her peace and satisfaction.

She'd changed so much since she'd come to Sunshine,

and she knew even more changes were in store—wonderful changes.

Together they sat watching the flames reaching into the autumn evening. The seasons were definitely moving from autumn to winter, and from the occasional touch of cold in the evening air, she knew that winter was making its steady way toward them.

Hayden raised her chin with a single finger and kissed her again. "I think," he said, his voice husky, "that I've wanted to do that from the first time I laid eyes on you, as you drove up in Trevor's truck, the horn blaring."

She smiled at the memory. "I had my book at my side. *The Complete Guide to Home Construction and Repair*—I thought it had everything I'd ever need in it."

"Where is it, by the way?"

"It's propping up the venting from the clothes dryer, which reminds me. I've got it taped together with aluminum tape, which I think works better than duct tape, but—"

The conversation lapsed into a discussion of the merits of the two kinds of tape, but it was punctuated with a kiss, and another kiss, and another kiss, until finally the fire died down and they were forced to rake it over and splash the coals with water from the bucket that was always nearby.

He walked her to the door of Sunshine. From the porch, she could hear the sound of the late-late show. Hayden squeezed her hand. "I need to get him and take him home. He's probably asleep in front of the tube."

"I doubt it. He's fascinated by it." She peeked through the screen door, and sure enough, the old man was in his chair, with Martha Washington curled into a gigantic furry ball on his lap.

"I gather Gramps is liking the new television," Hayden said, looking over her shoulder.

"He sure is. I don't think he'd ever seen a high-definition set, and now that I've got the satellite dish, he's been glued to it pretty much nonstop when he's out here during the day. Yesterday I caught him watching an infomercial about shoe inserts. Shoe inserts!"

Hayden shook his head in mock dismay. "Well, you've seen the disreputable things he wears on his feet. Maybe shoe inserts are exactly what he needs."

"I don't know. These have magnets in them."

"Why would there be magnets in shoe inserts?" he asked.

"You've got me. I have no idea. But if you want to ask Gramps, he can tell you, right down to the cost of shipping them to North Dakota. And if you buy two pairs, you get a free eye mask that's filled with a special herbal blend guaranteed to zap headaches, neuralgia, and insomnia."

"Sounds like you paid close attention." He moved in closer to her.

"I wasn't the one who did. Ask Gramps. I heard about it all through lunch. The afternoon treat was a talk show that featured some diet guru, and Gramps quizzed me about the gluten in the pasta I used and the amount of sugar in my cereal."

"What did you tell him?" Hayden's lips were very close to hers.

"I have no idea," she answered as she bridged the last inch between them.

She slid into the warmth that was his kiss, wanting nothing to ever come between them, wanting him to hold her in his arms for the rest of their days.

All her life, she'd been waiting for him. Hayden's

grandmother had been right.

"You know," Hayden said at last, when the embrace ended, "if I didn't need to breathe, I could stay here forever."

She smiled at him. He had the greatest eyes she had ever seen, the light blue of long-ago Nordic ancestors.

"No you couldn't. You need to go home," she said.

"I'll have to tear myself away." He ran his fingers down her cheek.

"You think that's going to be hard? Try getting Gramps away from his show. He's addicted to that television."

"I am not deaf!" the old man yelled from inside the house. "I have selective hearing, so I might not have heard any of those courting cooing things you said to each other, but on the other hand, maybe I did. So there, Grub."

Hayden's expression was shocked. "You did not!"

Livvy could hear the sounds of his grandfather pulling himself to his feet, apologizing to the cat as he did so— "Sorry, Martha, have to stand up"—and shuffling to the door. He grinned at the two through the screen.

"Look at you two, just as cozy as kittens on the hearth. I know what I know. I may be old but I know what's in front of my face, and I have to say that I am just tickled beyond belief."

"Gramps," Hayden said with an amused sigh, "you've got the cart way before the horse. You've taken a kiss and blown it into a marriage with two-point-five children and a white picket fence and—"

"Excuse me," Livvy interrupted before it could go any further, "did either of you happen to remember that I'm still here?"

"Oh, the kiss-ee," Gramps said.

She had to end this conversation—and quickly. "I am going to kick the both of you out of here so that you can go back to your own home, and Martha Washington and Leonard and I can get some sleep before one of us has to drive into town tomorrow morning for church. Good night."

Lightheartedly she kissed both men on the cheek, called to Leonard to come inside, and stood at the door watching the taillights of Hayden's truck as it left Sunshine.

She'd been kissed. By Hayden. And suddenly life, which had been extremely good before, took on a whole new shine of wonder.

eight

The first flakes of snow fell slowly, tiny bits of frozen sky and cloud that initially melted upon arrival, but then clung to the earth in the shadowed corners where the wind sent them. Hayden looked out the window and sighed.

"And we've got winter," Gramps said behind him.

Hayden wrapped his hands around his coffee cup, as if he could store the extra warmth for the trip out to the old resort.

He'd never been this tired in his life. Between shuttling back and forth, Obsidian to Sunshine to Obsidian to Sunshine to Obsidian, he had to fit in time to do his job in the schools and to grade assignments, talk to students, visit with parents, and serve on endless committee after endless committee.

Plus he felt that he had to constantly watch Gramps, even more so after what had happened the weekend before, when Gramps had decided to scramble some eggs, but then had gone to sleep in the chair at the kitchen table. The smoke detector had saved the apartment from a sure fire, but the alarm had nearly given Gramps a heart attack. They'd ended up in the hospital in Bismarck, with the old man hooked to monitors and machines that bleeped and blipped out endless electronic messages.

The image of Gramps in the bed, his frail and bent frame nearly lost in the white sheets and the wires clipped to his body, haunted Hayden. He'd come so close to losing him this time.

He couldn't leave him alone during the week, so the trips in the morning and the afternoon out to Sunshine had become crucial. Livvy had become a literal lifesaver. At least when Gramps was out there, he knew that his grandfather was safe.

He suspected it wasn't fair to Livvy, but she insisted she enjoyed the company, and he kept Martha Washington and Leonard occupied and out from under her feet.

Still though, still. . .

The doctor had stopped just short of an assessment of Alzheimer's. There were other possible causes of confusion, he'd told Hayden, and he'd discussed the variety of medications the old man was on. Gramps was now on a new regimen of pills and potions, and Hayden was supposed to monitor him constantly to determine if he was better—or worse—with the changed dosages.

It was too early to tell, and Hayden felt as if a heavy blanket of care was draped firmly and perpetually over his shoulders.

Even church, which had always been a source of renewal and strength for him, had become a chore. It had become one more thing in a long string of things. At night, when he finally wrapped himself in his old Cowboy Andy sleeping bag and curled up on the too-small sofa, he tried to say his prayers, but the words wouldn't sort themselves out of the swirling mass of all that he had to do.

He knew that God was aware of how much was on his plate right now, and that He saw through the garbled petitions of a tired man.

Here it was, Sunday morning, and he didn't even want to go to church. More than anything, he wanted to stay here, wrap himself in a nice warm throw, and read or watch television or sleep. He knew he'd benefit from the renewal that church gave him, but the thought of actually going through the process of getting ready for worship and then going there before he could profit from the service made him even wearier.

He had to admit it. He was exhausted.

He didn't resent any of it. Not at all. He was just tired. So tired.

Gramps's gnarled fingers touched his arm. "I know where the snowblower is," he said. "I'd better get it ready. Once the snow starts, it'll never stop."

He held back an impatient sigh. "We don't need the snowblower here. The apartment manager takes care of that. You know him. Joe, from the Cenex station? It's one of the advantages of living in the big city of Obsidian."

Gramps looked at him as if he'd begun spouting off multiplication tables in Portuguese. "Who said anything about bringing the snowblower here?" he asked. "I know Joe does all that. I'm talking about getting the one at Sunshine ready. And attaching the blade to the truck."

His grandfather had a good point. Hayden had always put off those two tasks.

The snowblower was an obstinate machine that required vast amounts of effort to get it to start—Hayden remembered with dismay how his arm would ache after he pulled the starter cord on it over and over and over, trying to get the motor to catch, and finally, when he was ready to give up, the dumb thing would finally engage.

Whether or not it would stay running until he was through snow-blowing the walkways from the house to the chicken coop and the barn was another matter entirely.

It was a cantankerous and belligerent piece of work, and Hayden dreaded approaching it after every snowfall.

Putting the blade on the truck was equally painful—often literally. He'd never made it without getting several gashes on his arms and hands, and one year he'd nearly sliced off his toe. He always wore steel-toed boots after that when dealing with the blade.

It was an awkward proposition, getting the blade attached to the front of the truck, but it had to be done. Usually Gramps helped him, but would he be able to this year? He had no idea.

Hayden created a smile and pasted it on. "You're right. I don't think this snow is going to stick, but let's not take a chance."

"We'll go out after church," his grandfather said.

Church. His entire Saturday had been eaten up with a three-hour practice for the boys' basketball team at school, followed by a trip to the grocery store, running Gramps out to Sunshine to get his afternoon medication that he'd forgotten there, staying to fix a board that had come loose in the living room flooring, going back to Obsidian and fixing dinner, grading twenty-seven algebra exams and sixteen geometry worksheets, washing a load of sheets and changing the bed, and more that he'd mercifully forgotten.

Now this was Sunday, and he so desperately wanted a day of rest. Wasn't that what it was all about? A day of rest?

"You'd better start getting ready for church. All I have left is to comb my silvery locks," Gramps said, running his hand over his thinning hair.

A battle of wills began to rage inside him. His body begged for some downtime, but his soul needed some up time, an hour spent with the Lord.

God would understand. He'd—

Hayden took one look at his grandfather, who was already in his suit, his tie neatly knotted, if a bit askew, and his face shining eagerly, and he knew that the decision was made.

He'd go with the up time.

As he headed for the shower, perhaps not with the enthusiasm he usually felt on Sunday mornings, Gramps called out from the kitchen, "Hey, Grub, Livvy will be there."

Hayden stopped, midstep, and shook his head. His grandfather was never going to stop matchmaking with the two of them. And, he admitted to himself as he continued his ascent up the stairs, he wasn't sure he wanted Gramps to quit.

Children were scurrying around the front of the church, gathering the snow in their mittens and alternately eating it or dumping it on top of each other's head. Hayden grinned as he watched them. It hadn't been that long ago that he'd done those same things himself. He lingered outside, enjoying the antics of the youthful churchgoers.

Soon though, watchful parents pulled their children inside, and he followed. Gramps had already gotten himself settled with some of the other old-timers, but he stood up and hobbled over to sit with Hayden.

"You know," Hayden said to him in the moments before the service started, "you've really got to get better boots. Those things you're wearing have not only seen better days, they've seen better decades."

Gramps shook his head. "They don't make them like they used to."

Hayden started to respond but Gramps interrupted,

standing up as quickly as he could and moving into the aisle. "Livvy!"

He also jumped up, banging his knee into the hymnal rack.

Livvy looked like the spirit of snow herself. Her face glowed crimson from the cold, which made her eyes sparkle with an even brighter deep brown.

"I'm freezing," she said as she slid down the pew next to Hayden, and Gramps followed her, so she had one on each side of her. "I know it's not really that cold, but the wind just cuts through me."

"It does that," Gramps said. "You're wise to wear a scarf, but you need something more substantial than that." He motioned to the airy chiffon scarf she had draped around her neck, and she laughed.

"This is just for vanity, Gramps," she said. "I have one that's out there in the entryway, keeping my coat company, that would keep out arctic breezes, let me tell you. My mom sent it from Sweden. No breeze is getting through it, trust me."

The service started, and Hayden let the words lift his cares from him.

Reverend Carlisle's theme was "Coming Home," based on, he explained, the upcoming set of holidays. As winter comes onto the starkness of the Badlands, it begins with a feast, a celebration of what has come before. The harvest, he pointed out, is the culmination of a busy season of planting, tending, and caring, before the reaping begins. The banquet is the ultimate festivity.

He leaned across the pulpit and grinned at the congregation. "Think how often we meet over food. We commemorate birthdays with a cake. Graduations, at least here in Obsidian, are marked with open houses and tray upon tray of bars and cookies and chips and dips. Weddings not only include a spectacular wedding cake, but a reception or perhaps a dinner. Even funerals end with us gathering over food."

Gramps's stomach growled, and Hayden and Livvy exchanged quick smiles.

"So we do as the song so known at Thanksgiving reminds us to do: We gather and we ask the Lord to bless us. And of course, we do this over as much food as we can possibly prepare," the minister continued. "And that leads us into what's commonly known as the holiday season, and if you look at the magazine display down at Grocery World, you'll see that probably ninety percent of the magazines offer tips on how to avoid gaining weight in this time period."

Reverend Carlisle patted his stomach. "As you can see, I am not an avid reader of these magazines."

The congregation laughed.

"Let me give you the gospel now. It's John 16:32: 'Behold, the hour cometh, yea, is now come, that ye shall be scattered, every man to his own, and shall leave me alone: and yet I am not alone, because the Father is with me.' Why, you might wonder, am I choosing this text, which talks about us being apart, not coming together? Because, my friends, it's simply this: It's easier to talk about the happy, feel-good things— what we used to call warm fuzzies back in the ancient world—but what we need to discuss is the time when those end. When we're in the January of our holiday season."

He must be more tired than he realized, Hayden thought. None of this was making sense. Why was Reverend Carlisle talking about the holidays so early, and now he was on to

January?

"I want you to see this as a continuum. It's beginning now. I know that some of you are, in fact, getting ready for the winter ahead. You came in through it. Winter starts early out here; you know that. And we tear through its beginnings thinking only of celebration and gathering and togetherness. But January does come. In our lives, it'll come. The time when there aren't parties and cookies and punch. Don't think of what you've lost. Think of what you've gained in these last days of autumn, what you've stored away just as surely as the squirrel stores its acorns. These are the things you will feed on in January."

Scattered. That's what was going to happen. He had put off answering the letter from the school district in Florida, perhaps under the misguided notion that the offer would simply evaporate and he wouldn't have to deal with it, but the superintendent had called him on Friday afternoon, asking for a definitive answer.

He could go to Florida, and even take Gramps with him. Sunshine was now in fantastic shape, and Livvy could open it in the spring without his help. He could try life in the big city, and see if his career path could actually have an arc in it instead of a flat line.

He could, but he didn't want to. He knew what his answer was going to be.

He knew.

When he got home, he would write a letter to that school, turning down the job—and choosing love.

&

The holidays sped by on winged feet. Thanksgiving gave way to Christmas, which bowed to the new year. And through it all, Livvy kept working, sending out flyers, calling travel agents, attending a travel agency gathering in Los Angeles. She'd even found a company in Valley City that would supply more orange T-shirts and blue glasses, just like the old ones.

She was determined to make this work.

And it seemed as if was going to. The phone began to ring. E-mails trickled in at first, and then increased. When she went to the mailbox, there were envelopes, some filled with requests for more information, others containing reservations and checks.

The brochure said it all:

Sunshine.
   An old-fashioned resort with old-fashioned values.
   We're experts at relaxation. Fish, play games, roast marshmallows, all in the safe and loving haven of North Dakota's stunning Badlands.
   No phones. No Internet. No cable.
   Just land and water. . .and you.
   Take it easy, here in Sunshine.
   And, as we've said for generations:
   At the end of the day, there's Sunshine.

But the test was going to be summertime. And when summer came, so did the guests. The cabins were full and the shouts of happy children combined with the songs at the bonfire every night, with Gramps leading the vespers. She was surprised at how quickly Sunshine's reputation grew, as a place where Christian families—or any family wanting an easy, comfortable setting—could spend a vacation.

Now it was August, and the season had been a smashing success. Livvy had had several requests to winterize the cabins so the resort could be open year-round, and she was considering it—even if her trusty *Complete Guide to Home Construction and Repair* wouldn't quite be up to the task.

Trevor had upgraded his rattletrap truck to a huge SUV and was now the official transport to the Bismarck airport—and had, indeed, managed to get a new iPod.

Her parents had come from Sweden and left with a new hobby—fishing.

Best of all, Gramps was much better. The doctor's suspicions had been right: The old man's confusion was the result of a drug interaction. Gramps was now as lively and alert as any teenager.

Life was good here in Sunshine, Livvy thought. Very good. And it was all because of what God had done. This was her inheritance—an inheritance of family and friends and love.

Hayden arrived with a delivery from Grocery World, and as they were putting it away in the kitchen, he commented on the success of Sunshine.

"I couldn't have done it without you," she said, and as she turned around, he caught her in a surprise embrace.

"Do you know what else you can't do without me?" he asked. "This."

He kissed her, squarely on the lips. "Let's put the ice cream away. I want to show you something down by the lake."

"Why? Is something wrong?" she asked, a crease of worry working its way up.

"Nothing's wrong, but it's something I think you should see."

She hurriedly put the ice cream in the freezer, and left the nonperishables on the counter.

"Come on," he said. "Come with me."

He took her by the hand and led her out of the house. Leonard followed them, his tennis ball in his mouth, and behind the dog came Martha Washington, her tail plumed as the chicken chased her, biting at her. Hayden shook his head and muttered, but he was smiling.

"What's this about?" she asked.

"Well," he said, pausing at the spot where the path opened to the lake, "I wanted a place where we might have some peace and quiet, but I didn't include the critters in the equation. And there's Gramps, out there on the dock. Well, so much for privacy. That's all right."

"What are you talking about?"

Hayden took her hands. "Livvy, I love you. I love everything about you, and I love the way I feel when I'm around you. You're the one that God has meant for me, I'm sure of that. Livvy—"

He dropped to one knee, and Leonard raced over and dropped his spit-covered tennis ball at his feet. "Not now, Leonard."

The dog nudged him, nearly knocking him over, and Livvy had to cover her mouth to keep from laughing. Hayden was so serious, but Leonard was insistent.

"Okay. Here." Hayden threw the ball and wiped his hands on his pants. "Quickly, before the beast comes back, Livvy, will you marry me?"

"I will! I will!" She knelt, too, landing squarely on the chicken, which flew upward in a great display of feathers and offended squawks, and landed on Martha Washington's back. The cat shot straight up into the air, and Leonard, seeing the great game at hand, joined in the fray.

She heard none of it. She only knew that Hayden was kissing her.

"I knew it," Gramps said from the pier, where he was fishing. "I knew it."

❧

The wedding was an autumn celebration, with Trinity decorated in the colors of the season. Bo and Al were their miniature groomsmen, and Bo flung the contents of his basket of multicolored leaves with such force that several guests were picking them out of their hair.

Gramps was there, as were her parents, and a surprise guest joined them from Boston: Mr. Evans, who gave them as a wedding present a copy of the advertisement, now framed. How he had gotten hold of it, she had no idea, but some things about love are simply magic.

Like Sunshine.

A Letter To Our Readers

Dear Reader:

In order that we might better contribute to your reading enjoyment, we would appreciate your taking a few minutes to respond to the following questions. We welcome your comments and read each form and letter we receive. When completed, please return to the following:

Fiction Editor
Heartsong Presents
PO Box 719
Uhrichsville, Ohio 44683

1. Did you enjoy reading *Sunshine* by Janet Spaeth?
   ❏ Very much! I would like to see more books by this author!
   ❏ Moderately. I would have enjoyed it more if

   _____

   _____

   _____

2. Are you a member of **Heartsong Presents**? ❏ Yes ❏ No
   If no, where did you purchase this book? _____

   _____

3. How would you rate, on a scale from 1 (poor) to 5 (superior), the cover design? _____

4. On a scale from 1 (poor) to 10 (superior), please rate the following elements.

   ____ Heroine   ____ Plot
   ____ Hero   ____ Inspirational theme
   ____ Setting   ____ Secondary characters

5. These characters were special because? _____

_____

_____

6. How has this book inspired your life? _____

_____

_____

7. What settings would you like to see covered in future
   Heartsong Presents books? _____

_____

_____

8. What are some inspirational themes you would like to see
   treated in future books? _____

_____

_____

9. Would you be interested in reading other **Heartsong
   Presents** titles?   ❏ Yes   ❏ No

10.   Please check your age range:
        ❏ Under 18   ❏ 18-24
        ❏ 25-34   ❏ 35-45
        ❏ 46-55   ❏ Over 55

Name _____

Occupation _____

Address _____

City, State, Zip_____

E-mail _____

Presents

Great Inspirational Romance
at a Great Price!

Heartsong Presents books are inspirational romances in contemporary and historical settings, designed to give you an enjoyable, spirit-lifting reading experience. You can choose wonderfully written titles from some of today's best authors like Wanda E. Brunstetter, Mary Connealy, Susan Page Davis, Cathy Marie Hake, Joyce Livingston, and many others.

When ordering quantities less than six, above titles are $3.99 each.
Not all titles may be available at time of order.

HEARTSONG
PRESENTS

If you love Christian romance...

$12.^{99}

You'll love Heartsong Presents' inspiring and faith-filled romances by today's very best Christian authors...Wanda E. Brunstetter, Mary Connealy, Susan Page Davis, Cathy Marie Hake, and Joyce Livingston, to mention a few!

When you join Heartsong Presents, you'll enjoy four brand-new, mass-market, 176-page books—two contemporary and two historical—that will build you up in your faith when you discover God's role in every relationship you read about!

Imagine...four new romances every four weeks—with men and women like you who long to meet the one God has chosen as the love of their lives...all for the low price of $12.99 postpaid.

Mass Market 176 Pages

To join, simply visit www.heartsong presents.com or complete the coupon below and mail it to the address provided.